Die Tante Band 1
by Johanna Schopenhauer
translated from the German
by LM Thaler

English translation
The Aunt (Part 1)
copyright ©2022 by LMS Books
Cover image ©2022 by LMS Books

L M S   B O O K S

CONTENTS

CHAPTER 1

One blustery fall evening, Babet and Agathe, two very pretty sixteen and seventeen year-old girls sat together feeling most discouraged. Outside, a vicious storm was whipping the rain fiercely against the windows, making the glass rattle against the frames and in the adjoining room, Victorine lay seriously ill. She was the only daughter of the wealthy merchant Kleeborn.

Since the early death of their parents, responsibility for the poor orphans had fallen to Kleeborn, who happened to be their mother's brother.

Even though they did not have any special restrictions regarding their sick relative, still the two girls did not feel like engaging in their customary free and high-spirited chats. The last two weeks had crept by so slowly. No balls to attend! No theatre for amusement! In fact, this was the first time in over a year, at least since the day that they had come from the boarding house to their uncle's home, that they found themselves completely deprived of any sort of entertainment.

Even though the evening had just begun, they had nothing interesting to say to each other and would have preferred just to go straight to bed, out of sheer boredom. But this was impossible because this particular evening it was their turn to watch over their cousin. Both were embarrassed to openly display their uneasiness otherwise each would have retreated to a corner to have a good cry.

After sitting there quite miserable for a while, they gradually got up and crept on tip toes around the room, taking care not to make any noise until Babet came to a stop at the window. She touched her pretty nose with her delicate finger.

Pausing a little, with an almost heroic sense of propriety, she cried:

"Right! The dark one!"

Overcome with curiosity and not thinking about the prevailing darkness, Agathe rushed towards her sister, bumping her head against the window in the process. The glass panes rattled with the impact.

"That was a beastly thing to do!" whimpered Agathe, rubbing her sore forehead. "I don't even know what you are looking for," she added.

"And I don't know what it has to do with you," answered Babet.

"What? And weren't you just telling me something about *the dark one*?" argued Agathe.

But Babet maintained that she had done no such thing and the discord between them started all over again. Just like the evening before, they began to squabble passionately with each other out of pure boredom.

Both shed a few impetuous tears as the dispute continued, until Babet sobbed: "This is just too much! Can't someone wonder out loud which hat to wear at church tomorrow without causing all this commotion?"

"What? Which hat to wear?" asked Agathe immediately in good spirits once more.

"Dear Babet! I really believed that you saw the *dark one* outside. Oh you know exactly the person I am talking about. That handsome dark-haired lieutenant!"

Suddenly overcome with an uncontrollable urge to laugh, the girls stopped crying instantly. The warning cough from the old French *Mamsell,* signalling like an approaching thunderstorm was in vain because the girls could not stop laughing. Even *Mamsell's* stern whisper "Children, please!" as she came through the door could not dampen their spirits. They stuffed their cambric handkerchiefs into their pretty little mouths but it was all to no avail. Finally, still giggling the girls nestled so closely into their uncle's enormous easy chair that their curly locks almost blended together.

It was getting dark since no one had thought to illuminate the room. The wind howled in the chimney and whistled sharply through the long corridors of the spacious house. Despite their laughter, the girls were a little apprehensive. They did not want to get up just yet, so they stayed put and began to chat about matters dear to their hearts. After all, it was the perfect time for a little discussion.

"Tell me," whispered Agathe, "Does he come to church when you wear your black hat?"

"Heaven forbid! But like everyone else, he waits in front of the church every Sunday to watch the ladies as they come in and he always greets me in a most peculiar fashion. But he hasn't seen me in the black hat yet since it is still too new. Still, the black hat suits me best, as you know. Oh dear! I haven't seen poor Theodor for eight days now!" responded Babet with a rather pitiful sigh.

"If only the holidays didn't go by so quickly! Soon he will have to go back to Göttingen," she added. "All that silly studying! And Monday there's a new opera and Tuesday there's the ball at the Casino! What use is it to be engaged for the first waltz, or for the second quadrille[1] and cotillion[2]? Everyone envied me then! But I am so unhappy now!"

"Yes, that's so sad," reflected Agathe, "and that's why I will never fall in love. Never in my entire life!"

"I hardly think so!" chuckled Babet. "You don't want to end up an old maid, like our aunt, do you?"

"Oh, our dear dignified aunt! Let's not talk about her!" responded Agathe suddenly annoyed. "I wish that she would go jump in the lake, or go back to where she came from. Our uncle didn't really need to send for her because of Victorine. I'm sure that we could have managed taking care of our cousin and nursed her back to health without our aunt's help. Of course, I don't know our aunt all that well . . ."

"I don't know her either," interrupted Babet. "But she will be just as awkward with me as she is with you. Just watch! She will be extremely bossy and demanding with us. As if we didn't have enough problems already with *Mamsell!* She isn't even our *real* aunt anyway, since Mother was Uncle Kleeborn's natural sister and Aunt is simply the sister of his late wife. On top of everything, she is a nun or some such equivalent!"

"Actually, she is a *canoness*[3] interjected Agathe, pedantically. "Oh, we will deal with her somehow. But let's get back to our discussion about that certain dark-haired individual. You see, I am only pretending to be interested in him because I believe that I must participate on a social level, since I am part of this world, but I will never marry him, even if he proposes. Upon my honour!"

After this announcement, Agathe very solemnly leaned back in the arm chair, looking so funereal that Babet burst out laughing.

"Do you really know him all that well?" she asked.

"Perish the thought! I only meant if I knew him, answered Agathe. Actually I do know him. You know how often we have danced together and he has even visited the Obrists next door twice already. I heard every word he said, and I can assure you he spoke very respectably."

"Oh, did you visit the Obrists, then? asked Babet. "You never told me this."

"Well, not exactly," replied Agathe. "I urgently needed to see Amelie about the money bag that I am crocheting for Uncle's Christmas present. So I stood at the door for a while."

"I see," said Babet thoughtfully. I just wish that my Theodor would finally speak with Uncle. Actually, he will be finished with his studies by Easter. By Pentecost[4] he will have his examinations and on St. John's Day[5] he will be employed . . ."

"And then marry you on Michaelmas[6]! You have your life all planned out in quarterly instalments," interrupted Babet with a giggle.

"Mistress Aunt has arrived!" announced a servant passing quickly by their room and both girls hurried to compose themselves so that they could meet their dreaded aunt with a confidence that they did not really feel.

A tall, slender, awe-inspiring figure in close-fitting black travelling clothes stood in the marble-panelled hallway, surrounded by servants holding candles, ready to lead her into the room that had been prepared for her. The black clothes and the white cap with the black-laced veil made her appear quite nun-like. The noble, somewhat sharply defined features of the pale face still bore the unmistakable traces of a former rare beauty. Her fine lips and still beautiful mouth were as eloquent as eyes were for other people, curiously expressing every fleeting emotion. At first sight, her large blue eyes seemed colourless and nondescript, but they radiated with an inner glow as the aunt spoke. One had to admit that she was certainly stunning. Her eyes, shadowed by long dark lashes hinted at something both romantic and idealistic, recalling beautiful images of the *Mater dolorosa*[7] that we still see in old churches sometimes.

The aunt appeared to be hardly fifty years of age, although she was in fact almost ten years older and the proud bearing of this tall woman had not yet bowed to the hands of time. Traces of advancing maturity were almost imperceptible in the soft blond hair. In fact, nature had been gentle with her and had allowed this rare masterpiece to be preserved from the ravages of time for as long as possible.

Certainly this vision of beauty was not what Agathe and Babet had expected. With some embarrassment and a little trepidation, they accompanied her to her room, respectfully following behind her, as if she were royalty. Although both girls had spoken of her rather presumptuously just a few minutes ago, now they felt intimidated by her presence. Only furtively they stole glances at the very pretty, pallid and obviously exhausted girl that was that was leaning against their aunt.

"Uncle is not home, but we will send for him straightaway," stammered Agathe.

"He is at the Casino. He goes there every evening for his entertainment and generally only comes home after midnight," added Babet, somewhat emboldened.

"Please don't disturb him, I will speak with him tomorrow," responded the aunt politely. "For now I would like to see *Mamsell* Virnot, so that she can enlighten me concerning Victorine's condition. But you, my dear nieces . . . you are my nieces, aren't you?"

"Of course! We're Babet and Agathe," the girls cried out in chorus.

"Well then, dear Babet and Agathe, may I introduce my foster child? Her name is Angelika. I don't ask that you love her because that will certainly happen all by itself. You may begin by accepting her with kindness and helping the poor travel-weary child to get some rest."

CHAPTER 2

It was now past midnight and Victorine was sleeping soundly, breathing quietly. The doctor, who had come late in the evening, had given them hope for steady recovery.

Agathe and Babet had gone to bed a few hours before. Their aunt, who was not at all tired from her trip, had insisted upon relieving them of their duties regarding the ailing Victorine.

"Young girls need to rest," she explained to her old friend Virnot, referring to her two sleepy nieces.

"Adolescents need sleep in order to grow. Just as a blossoming flower needs the dew to refresh itself. It's different with us. As we approach the autumn of our lives, nature becomes frugal and teaches us to carefully budget the limited hours that may still be allotted to us."

The aunt was sitting in the little room next to where Victorine lay sleeping, in the same armchair where a few hours ago, Babet and Agathe had discussed their little problems of the heart. Across from her, *Mamsell* Virnot was diligently knitting by the dimming light. The door to the adjoining room was open, and the two guardians were alert to any movement, but Victorine was sound asleep.

"My dear Virnot," began the aunt in a soft whisper. "My dear old loyal friend, I must take advantage of this first opportunity without interruption to speak with you alone, so that I may thank you for the love and kindness you have shown my poor Victorine."

"Oh that dear child!" replied the French woman cheerfully. "I feel as though she were my own child. *Je l'ai vu naître*; these arms have carried her since infancy; how could I not love her? *C'est un coeur excellent*, a little tempestuous, a little arrogant sometimes, but that is just her youth. The reason for this is actually quite admirable. *C'est le vrai portrait de feu Madame sa mère*. When I compare Babet and Agathe with her! Oh, my dear lady! *Ces chers Enfants* are a pair of malicious little brats."

"You don't really mean that!" said the aunt with a smile. "Maybe they are a little naughty sometimes, but they aren't spiteful. Adolescents are rarely, if ever, truly hateful. But I would like to talk about our Victorine. It's been twelve years now, since I have seen either her or her father and here I am, in the midst of my own, as if among strangers. And yet . . . with all my heart, I love this beautiful reflection of my dear sister who passed away so prematurely. The last time I saw her she was a child of six and now she is a young woman of eighteen."

"And how she has changed, *cette chère petite Victorine!*" added the governess. "*Belle comme le jour, Madame, je vous assure.* Before she became ill, not one of young *Demoiselles* could hold a candle to her; she was the epitome of loveliness, and now . . . *hélas!*"

"She will be so again, dear Virnot," reassured the aunt.

"Oh *Madame*, sighed the governess. I am so worried that doctor will not be able to do much for our Victorine because the only thing that can cure her cannot be found at the apothecary shop. If only she had trusted me, but she kept silent and cried to herself, and now she is lying here."

"Dear Virnot, you are alarming me!" cried the aunt. "Please tell me everything you know or suspect concerning the precious child, never mind how little or insignificant it may seem to you. It is absolutely necessary that I am reasonably prepared so that I can win Victorine's trust. I hope that she will have a place in her heart for me and that she can learn to love me for her mother's sake, even though she knows me only from letters that were exchanged all too rarely. Unfortunately I was never very well-acquainted with Victorine's surroundings and therefore I never had much influence on her life. In this house, I really only know you, dear Virnot and I appreciate the loyalty you have shown over the years to my sister and her child. All others are strangers to me, even Victorine's father. We never really became close to each other. But the love of my sister's only child could encourage me to exchange the solitude that I love for life in this noisy city, at least for a while."

"*Et Dieu en soit loué mille fois*!" cried the honest Virnot. "Because more than ever, this household requires someone like yourself to head it, dear lady. Only you can provide proper direction to our *Demoiselle*. After all, I was always just her servant. While I was not actually born in France, rather in the French community in Berlin, she did learn French from me. *Madame, elle parle comme une petite Parisienne!* She has acquired just the right accent. *Eh bien*, God's gift to her. And she has a certain poise . . . certain manners. Just like a princess! But all this is not enough*, maintenant qu'elle est une grande Demoiselle*, I cannot accompany the child everywhere she goes. And besides, I have the household duties to contend with as well, so it is most fortunate that you, Madame, will accept this responsibility regarding your niece."

"Dear Virnot, before we continue, I must ask you to refrain from addressing me with my official title. Outside of the convent and especially here, I find it most inappropriate. Now, tell me about what must be done and how I can help. What should be my main area of concern?"

"*Eh bien donc, Madame, vous le voulez,*" answered the governess as she removed her glasses and arranged herself in the easy chair. "*Au fond,*" she continued. "I believe that *cher Papa* is to blame for many of our problems. Master Kleeborn is certainly a good man who loves his child, just as a proper father should and must. Victorine lacks for nothing. He engages the most expensive tutors for all subjects essential to a young *Demoiselle*. His house is the most magnificent in the city. Oh, *Madame*, you would not believe the hurdles I face when I must prepare for our endless social events. Of course we have adequate servants, but the final responsibility lies on my shoulders, *mais je le fais de bon coeur*. Yes, what I wanted to say, to return to our topic. Yes, our *jeune Demoiselle* also has a wardrobe fit for a queen, *je vous assure*, jewelry and every accessory to complement her outfits. But this is of little consequence. After all, Master Kleeborn has a princely fortune. Everyone at the stock exchange respects him and he can well bear the burden. *Mais, Madame, entre nous soit dit,* this was not always the case. There was a time, not long before Mistress Kleeborn passed away, perhaps about ten years ago, that terrible time when Europe was teetering on its stilts, as Master Kleeborn says when he discusses those days. There must have been a dark cloud over the commercial world, because *figurez-vous, Madame,* in Amsterdam, in London, in every major commercial city the largest firms collapsed. An atmosphere of distrust dominated every activity, *plus de confiance, plus de crédit, nulle part*. Each day Master Kleeborn brought more bad news and he was always as pale as my handkerchief here when he brought letters that were directed to him into Mistress Kleeborn's room. He did this because he was afraid to open his mail at his office, in the presence of his employees. Very likely he was afraid to betray himself if confronted with bad news at an inopportune time. Of course, this did not stop the bad news from coming, and Master Kleeborn saw himself *au bord d'un précipice*, as the saying goes. He was not quite ruined, but he was in fact, *pour le moment*, in a very urgent financial difficulty and only an infusion of ready money could rescue him if he was to avert defaulting on his payments, the way so many others did then. *Le pauvre homme*! Just the thought of having to take such drastic measures reduced him to despair. My poor mistress suffered with him of course, because he was able to share his troubles only with her. *Ah! comme elle en a pleuré!*"

"My poor sister hid all of this from me!" sighed the aunt.

"I believe so," replied Virnot. "She never complained, but since that time there were few happy hours left for her. To console Master Kleeborn, she would tearfully suggest that he turn to her wealthy relative for help. In fact, she wrote a letter to her great uncle, the one who owns those sizable estates in Silesia.[8] In their distress, both the master and mistress turned to other affluent members of this aristocratic family. Your grace is certainly better acquainted with the names of these families and estates, *mais* . . . the compassionate narrator paused here, as if she were embarrassed to speak further, but the aunt appealed to her repeatedly until Virnot decided to continue.

"*Enfin, Madame, vous le voulez ainsi*," she began once again. "so I must sadly admit that one refusal followed another, though I must say the rejections were phrased most eloquently. *Madame*, I cannot describe to you the pitiful condition of my mistress under those circumstances. During this time, her husband's worries

15

were always her biggest concern, her own troubles were secondary. Unfortunately, however Master Kleeborn was not spared from reproaches concerning the behavior of their relatives, *et cependant, Dieu le sait, la pauvre chère femme n'en pouvait rien,* she endured everything in her most cheerful manner, but I think that at the time, every day was another nail in her coffin."

Old Virnot burst into tears, and the aunt began to cry as well. Finally, the kind woman composed herself. "Oh *Madame*," she sighed. *"nous avons bien souffert*, but finally help came from a source least expected by Master Kleeborn. This was a prosperous estate in Amsterdam, a family previously acquainted with Master Kleeborn's father. He had not approached this family, because even they had not been spared from blows in those financially catastrophic times. At a time when brothers did not trust one another, they sent Master Kleeborn large sums of money, and extended his credit of their own accord. The magnanimity of these business acquaintances rescued him and his financial situation remained intact. He was able to go to the stock exchange with his head held high, but this did not help my poor mistress and from that day on, he felt extremely hostile toward her family and the nobility. Incessantly he ridiculed the *bourgeoisie*[9] who were foolish enough to associate with the nobility, and he assured us that his Victorine—my God, *la pauvre petite* was barely seven years old at the time— that he would never surrender his daughter to anyone but a merchant. 'A true merchant,' he used to say 'has chosen the most respectable, useful and therefore most honourable profession.' Only a merchant can connect two hemispheres, only his sharp eye can detect shortages in the remotest countries, and when he nods, richly-laden ships speed from one pole to another to address these needs. His word, and his command means something in the old world as well as in the new and the stroke of his pen can set millions in currency and thousands of industrious hands in motion hundreds of miles away. *"Ne vous étonnez pas, Madame,"* that I can tell you all this, but I have heard this tirade so many times, in almost the same words that I have managed to learn it by heart. In concluding, Master Kleeborn would usually add 'Let a count or a baron or one of your aristocratic relatives try to find out what is worth more in a foreign country. A venerable name? A thousand year old family tree? Or my simple, barely fifty-year-old company. Martin Nikolaus Kleeborn, my personal signature. Emperors and kings look to us for refuge and we must help everyone, but when we need help and they foolishly look elsewhere . . .' Then the old song would start *et Madame pleurait!* Certainly it seemed to me that the Master was not entirely wrong but why endlessly repeat these offensive remarks to my mistress? *Aussi en avait elle le coeur navré,* but she would not tolerate a single word from me in her defense. Finally, six months later, she became so tired of life that she lay down and went to sleep forever. *Dieu aye pitié de son ame!"*

"Eh bien," resumed Virnot with trembling voice after a short pause. *"Eh bien,"* he cried to God and continues to do so, for he truly loved my dear mistress. At first, his conscience would plague him terribly, but with the hustle and bustle of business this was soon alleviated. Then several fortunate business transactions occurred. This is what they say at the stock exchange when a lot of money is made through speculation. Master Kleeborn's fortune increased from year to year and he became the millionaire he is today. While his house became ever more magnificent and stylish, at the same time Victorine, soul heiress to his fortune, grew to be the most beautiful *Demoiselle* in the city. And we would have balls, concerts, meetings, theatre, where respectable strangers of every rank and position were welcomed *et notre chère petite Victorine* looked like a little queen, *au beau milieu de tout cela."*

"Poor child," sighed the aunt.

17

"That's right!" agreed the housekeeper. "She was entirely alone, *dans ce tourbillion*, without a *chère Maman* to protect her. However, I must say to her credit that thousands of other young *Demoiselles* would have behaved quite differently had they been in her position. Our *Mademoiselle* Babet, for instance, *mais passons là-dessus*. Our Victorine was always polite and friendly to everyone, without pretensions of any kind. Suitors did not stay away for long and some had their eyes *on les beaux yeux de la cassette de son père* but that is the way of the world. There *were* enough counts and barons competing for *our petite Demoiselle*. There was even talk about a close relative with familial connections to royalty, *mais cela reste entre nous.* It was quite natural that Master Kleeborn would be happy about the accomplishments of his beautiful daughter, but he politely but very definitively dismissed all respectable offers that came her way. He maintained that his daughter would only marry a merchant, just as he was. Now, Madame, *nous voilà arrivé au point*, we have arrived at the point, I wanted to say, where . . ."

"What do you mean," asked the aunt, who was starting to get a little impatient.

"Well, at this point," replied Virnot. "the point at which Victorine's illness began. Dear Lord, I hope that I am mistaken. And that my premonitions do not come to pass, *mais j'ai un pressentiment bien triste au fond du coeur.* I am afraid that she has unfortunately fallen in love with a certain gentleman, one among those fine gentlemen who had unsuccessfully made proposals for her hand. And if her *cher papa* maintains his position, then just like her *pauvre chère maman . . .*"

"Take courage, dear Virnot!" interjected the aunt. "Do not automatically think the worst. A young heart does not break so easily, because it always holds on to the slightest hope. And hope does not let us perish so easily. But tell me, do you know this man whom you believe . . ."

"*Hélas non!* I don't know anyone," sighed the housekeeper a little reflectively before continuing in her usual chatty manner. "When society is there, I do not go into the salon. I have enough to do in the house to keep me busy, *c'est la mer à boire.* Truly, *Madame,* I would need a hundred eyes and just as many wings."

"I believe you, dear Virnot," replied the aunt. "But let us discuss Victorine."

"Oh *Madame,*" began the housekeeper. "*que voulez vous, que je vous en dise?* I don't know anything else, except that a short time before, her *Papa* requested her to come to his office. This did not really surprise me because it is his habit to discuss with Victorine her future proper conduct regarding any new suitor *en question* that he has rejected. This time she stayed in his office about an hour; much longer than usual. Finally, she returned to her room, *mais grand Dieu! dans quel état!* She was as pale as death, I tell you. At that moment, she looked just like her *pauvre maman!* When she threw her pretty arms around my old neck, she cried so sorrowfully. Not since the death of her poor mother, did she cry so much. I cried too, not really understanding why, but could I do otherwise? La *pauvre petite me perçoit le coeur.* Finally, I tried my best to console her, *mais,* dear God, how could I help her? She was so passionate, her eyes flashed wildly and she moved about so *égaré,* that I was paralysed with fear. *Quoi faire*? I did not know what to do. She cried, she reproached, and said all sorts of things that I was not able to interpret *comme j'ai eu l'honneur de le dire à Madame.* This lasted some time. She staggered about just a shadow of herself, writing letters, crying again and again until a violent fever robbed her strength and sense of reality. Since that time, she is lying here, *comme Madame l'a trouvée.* Today was critical, but the doctor was optimistic *et le bon Dieu en soit béni mille fois.* I think that the presence of her *chère Tante* is the best remedy for the poor girl. If she would only speak! To speak with her would be the best consolation!"

Although the aunt had listened to the old genial housekeeper with great interest, she was barely able to suppress a smile when she heard this last comment.

Meanwhile dawn had come, and the aunt left to make herself comfortable. Soon Victorine woke up, showing signs of recovery and from then on, the aunt tried to be with her whenever possible. Although the doctor had stated that Victorine's condition was no longer critical, she now required more attentive care than that time when she lay in that unconscious state, suspended between life and death. The doctor nevertheless cautioned that any excitement, joyful or not, could result in a serious relapse. So the aunt was very careful to maintain an atmosphere of uninterrupted tranquility for her niece and to avoid long conversations, regardless of how amusing they might be.

Angelika, too hovered about in the invalid's room almost inaudibly like a friendly guardian angel. Yet she never made a nuisance of herself among the hustle and bustle of activity surrounding Victorine. She read every appeal in Victorine's eyes fulfilling every need tenderly and graciously before it was expressed. Love and life were the same for this intensely sensitive creature but the sad melody of a lingering melancholy seemed to echo from deep within her. The name Angelika[10] seemed to have been invented for her, her inner beauty projected so perfectly in her physical form.

Since childhood, Angelika had experienced joy only vicariously, reflected in a second-hand way by observing the happiness in the eyes of other people. It was not maternal love that blanketed her cradle, because Angelika's birth had brought death to her mother and unified her once more with the husband who had died a few short weeks before.

Responsibility for Angelika's welfare was then subsequently assigned to paid guardians, since she lived in a small town near the Rhine[11] and her parents had only lived there a few months. Most people, including Angelika's guardian had heard of this town by name only. But the good reputation, confirmed by testimonials of his character assured Angelika's mother that her she could surrender the newborn child to this man for protection.

With the best of intentions, he brought his ward to a woman he assumed to be respectable and paid her a small sum of money for board. The modest estate left by Angelika's parents, he managed as advantageously as possible for her benefit.

Entrusted to this woman, Angelika attained her eighth year of age without faring too badly. Now her Guardian decided that she should go to school in France. He had an infinite passion for the country where he had spent his own youth and he was firmly convinced that a penniless girl like Angelika would learn the essentials required to eventually become a governess for the children of a prince or at least a paid companion for a lady of high rank so that she could advance in the world.

Unfortunately all the noted institutions in an around Paris were too expensive for Angelika's rather limited means, but her guardian's childhood friend who lived in *Angoulême*[12] recommended an inexpensive school with exceptionally high standards in that town.

The guardian was pleased to have found this fortunate solution for his young ward and since he had been coincidentally offered an opportunity to go there, he decided to accompany her there immediately.

So the poor orphan had to leave her homeland for one of the most desolate, bleak, and grimy towns in southern France. She would forfeit the springtime of her life to live among people who would always remain strangers to her, even long after she had learned their language.

She would learn that life here meant monastic constraints, even pleasure was ritualized. Three or four governesses and a strict school mistress reigned over a fairly large number of girls drawn from all over the world, including America.

In the school hierarchy, these governesses ranked below the head mistress. She controlled her subordinates with a powerful sceptre, and allowed herself to be slavishly worshipped by her subjects as if she were deity.

The students differed from each other significantly by homeland, language, talent and temperament. Yet they were all treated identically; all were subject to strict regimentation that seemed to have been conceived only to stifle any joyful emotion of a young mind.

Transplanted here, Angelika was like a neglected ivy among fragments of pottery, struggling in vain to extend its slender tendrils in all directions, seeking an object to embrace with devotion. An indefinable constant yearning took possession of her soul, but Angelika could not find even one person who would have found it worthwhile to accept the love she had to offer. There were acquaintances, but no friends and no one to whom she could say: "I belong with you." No one displayed the slightest compassion for Angelika.

CHAPTER 3

But time passes for the fortunate just as it does for the less fortunate and so the years flew by for Angelika, taking the joyless childhood away as well. Yet just as a flower rooted in rocky alpine soil is often more beautiful than its sister carefully tended in a garden, this lonely girl, accustomed only to harsh rules and deprivations of all kinds, did not grow up to be less beautiful than a happy one.

She had heard the word "love" only in a religious context. She had never read a novel, in fact she had little opportunity to read at all. She had never been to the theatre, nor had she ever seen a man, other than the teachers at the school. And those were all gray-haired men who thanked God when at the end of the day they were relieved of their bothersome duties. Still, a mysterious ideal floated into Angelika's imagination, her quiet fantasy was roused by something most beautiful. When she was asleep and even while awake, a lovely dream softened her life, making a world that was so alien to her a magical radiance, enfolding the lonely impoverished girl with a powerful wisdom. The rapture of absolute sacrifice and the premonition of the tender and infinite bliss of a pure love captured her young heart.

When Angelika turned sixteen years of age, her guardian decided that he would fetch her himself from *Angoulême* and accompany her to northern Germany to the home of a close relative of her late father, who had finally come to the conclusion that it would be a good idea to remind himself of the existence of his niece.

It had been planned that she would stay with this family for another year in order to learn the German language, manners and customs. This was necessary before Angelika could accept a position with a widowed princess who lived by herself; a position that her relatives were in the meantime still in the process of securing for their niece.

Angelika trembled with fearful anticipation as she entered the house where for the first time in her life she would meet people who bore her own family name and she believed that she had finally found the place where she belonged.

Determined that she would love her relatives dearly, unfortunately she would discover here too, her eager longing for affection would not be reciprocated. Her relatives offered only a cold measure of stiff formalities and Angelika shivered in response, just as a mimosa[13] reacts when the cold north wind blows.

Angelika realized immediately that she was perceived as a stranger here, with her foreign language, manners and clothing and would only be tolerated by them, but never loved.

She was a foreigner in their midst and by her appearance interpreted as someone belonging to a people that provoked every German heart and inspired every capable man to rise in revolt.

Despite outward appearances and all that had been forced upon her during her time at school, Angelika had never learned to love France. What did she know of France after all, other than the old dismal city where she had lived and the house where she had spent her childhood languishing in austere atmosphere of suppression? Everything else from that time had remained alien to her, even the name of the town.

Deep inside, Angelika had always yearned for her homeland all those years. She had held on to her childhood image, glorified by the magic gleam that distance and deprivation seem to make every object much brighter.

Secretly, she had tried very hard to preserve her mother tongue and had faithfully brought a few children's books with her to France when she had left her home town. These books were sacred to her. Whenever she had a spare moment to herself, she read out loud, only to hear the treasured cadence of her own language. She continued this practice even though her intellectual capacity soon advanced beyond the limits of this meagre library.

Thus prepared, it was not difficult for Angelika to re-adapt to her native German and it was not long before she was quite proficient in it once more. Living among these relatives she had not known before, the elegant manners of her people, and the beautiful natural surroundings that she had missed since childhood made her homeland all the more dear to her. But this acutely sensitive girl had to love it in her own way so that she could endure the hatred that was very prevalent wherever she went.

Angelika's return to her homeland occurred at that memorable time when every German soul was awakened by a spirit of heroism. A youthful fresh breeze reinvigorated a world that had been burdened for a very long time. Every heart beat with a sincere hope and Germany's confident young men rushed in every direction, discovering the lost homeland in the hospitality offered in every home.

This was how Ferdinand von Klarenau came to the house of Baron Sternwald, the home of Angelika's uncle and now her new home. Ferdinand was the first person who had immediately looked at Angelika with friendship and confidence, and the lonely girl who had longed for companionship all her life now believed she had found the ideal of all childhood dreams.

From that day forward, his presence changed Angelika's world, making it at once radiant and intensely beautiful. He was young and poetic and believed in this country and in justice and he shared the joyful enthusiasm that inspired him with Angelika. It seemed to her, that her real life only began on the day that she met Ferdinand. With every breath, Angelika gave thanks for the happiness that now filled a heart so unaccustomed to this almost overpowering joy.

Since conditions seemed to favour the two lovers, Angelika's relatives regarded him to be her betrothed when he left. She would extend her hand when returned from battle, for now the hope of victory blazed in his eyes, and the pain of their departing hour gently and quietly subsided. So Ferdinand left to fight for the woman he loved and Angelika stayed behind to pray for him.

CHAPTER 4

When he was gone, the poor girl never dreamed that he would not return, yet this is what happened. He joined the Lützow Free Corps.[14] Together with his courageous comrades, he would experience war with all its terrible treachery and destruction. What finally happened to him? Nothing was ever heard of him again, but one thing was certain. Dejected and demoralized, he had disappeared without a trace. Like so many who had fought with him only to die.

Like a nightingale who no longer sings when spring is gone, Angelika was alone now but never complained. Her life was a faint whisper and though she appeared serene to all, her every heartbeat was a never-ending death. Often it seemed to her that she was fighting a terrible dream and she would tearfully pray to God to rescue her from this dream. She did not want to believe the sad truth. But then the relentless pain in her breast returned and once again she had to accept the reality of her situation.

In their own way, the essentially kind-hearted people did everything they were capable of in order to comfort Angelika, but unintentionally they often wounded where they had sought to heal.

Finally, they brought her to Pyrmont,[15] in the hope that the stimulation of activities there would distract her, but soon they themselves were so preoccupied with the hustle and bustle of society, that they did not notice that the more boisterous and refreshing the ambiance, the more quiet and ashen-faced Angelika became.

And yet a good angel took pity on the suffering girl and brought her Victorine's Aunt, the Canoness Anna von Falkenhayn, who would be able to offer Angelika the only consolation left for her, the comfort of a truly sympathetic friend.

People who met Angelika generally felt compassionate towards the pale grieving girl, but in Anna's noble mind, the compassion was transformed to a natural and motherly affection. Angelika responded immediately to this outpouring of love with all the fervour which had always been a part of the unfulfilled hunger and torment of her life. In an instant, Miss Anna von Falkenhayn realized that the environment where her young friend lived could not possibly be beneficial for a broken heart.

Anna witnessed herself their attitude towards Angelika and the harsh fate that had caused this tender plant to wither. The somewhat jovial manner in which they took into their confidence not only Anna, but anyone else who was curious about Angelika was rather inappropriate, although her relatives were neither aware of this, nor did they wish to offend anyone. They meant well and wanted to help the poor girl, but communication between people who were in fact strangers to one another is always difficult.

Finally Anna von Falkenhayn, made a request that Angelika's relatives responded to and granted with great joy, because her condition had been deteriorating rapidly. In any case, the staff here could do nothing more for her and soon Angelika left with her new friend Anna to start a new life.

Anna von Falkenhayn treated her as if she were a daughter, caring for her with a profound tenderness as if she were trying to revive a sick flower.

With gracious and gentle care, Anna learned to love the suffering girl more each day and Angelika grew to depend on the kind-hearted presence of her guardian.

For Anna, it was unthinkable to leave her alone, even for a few months, and this was why the special girl who had become just like a beloved daughter, accompanied her to the Kleeborn household. Angelika, too, shared in her concern for Victorine.

It was not just Victorine, daily showing encouraging signs of recovery, who felt the sense of order and serenity that the aunt brought with her. In fact all members of the household felt the same way. Dear old Virnot was cheerful again, dashing up and down the stairs, carrying her collection of keys, keeping watch over her considerable regiment of female servants.

Even Babet and Agathe learned to appreciate both the aunt and Angelika, because their presence was like a breath of fresh air in the stifling sickroom. At last the girls were able to sit again by the window, evaluating passersby. There was so much for them to talk about and sometimes there were interesting people to greet, for example the dark-haired lieutenant and the blond Theodor, seemed to be very much engaged in the vicinity of the Kleeborn house because they appeared daily.

This preoccupation, as well as their contemplation of winter wardrobes when circumstances improved gave these two almost inexhaustible material for their entertainment, so disputes and bad tempers were set aside for now.

Master Kleeborn, on the other hand, felt somewhat depressed by his sister-in-law's presence, which was odd since he had requested her visit in the first place. But he would never admit his uneasiness to anyone.

Her almost exaggerated delicacy with which she reacted to trivialities, her strict adherence to discretion in all family matters and her somewhat old-fashioned attitude concerning decency and decorum made him feel embarrassed and apprehensive whenever she was near. It did not escape him that Anna von Falkenhayn was able to able to control the entire household including himself without ever having to utter a single command.

All members of the household adjusted their behaviour according to the expression on Anna's face and it seemed to everyone, from the most menial position among the servants to the master of the household, that it could not be otherwise.

"Those cursed stuffy aristocratic mannerisms," thought Kleeborn. At least he tried thinking about this, but on the whole he did not have the courage to talk with Anna about matters which she did not want to hear about. She wanted to get to know Victorine better, before discussing Kleeborn's intentions concerning his daughter.

Kleeborn, on the other hand, didn't take Victorine's illness all that seriously and had actually used it as a pretext for inviting his sister-in-law. His actual intention however was to exert his influence over his daughter and make her more inclined to see his way through her aunt. Meanwhile, he felt that Anna's presence was essential to heighten the splendour and grandeur of the many festivities which he hoped would soon coincide with Victorine's recovery as well as the fulfilment of his plans. For next to making money there was nothing that Kleeborn loved more than surrounding himself with glory and splendour and challenging the most distinguished people. Despite his loudly proclaimed contempt for innate nobility, he nevertheless counted himself lucky to have among his close relatives a woman of Anna von Falkenhayn's rank and reputation.

With satisfaction he often regarded her majestic figure and the stately poise displayed in every gesture and rejoiced in advance for the moment when she would honour his home by wearing that impressive habit of her religious order, embellished by the large diamond cross. This was the same outfit that she wore in her vocation as canoness.

He consoled himself with the faith that what was postponed was not cancelled and that after Victorine's full recovery, he would find an opportune moment to win over the aunt. For the time being, with perfect peace of mind, he accepted that his usual after-work amusements would have to take place outside his home. It was impossible for him to relax in his own home when Victorine was in this mournful condition.

Victorine was feeling remarkably well and the bright morning sunshine on this clear autumn morning had tempted the Aunt and Angelika to go outside.

Müller, the old bookkeeper, was about to exit through the front door when the two returned from their walk. As she had not yet met the old gentleman since her arrival at the Kleeborn household, the aunt hastened her steps so that she could chat with him a little. She had known him for a long time and respected him as her brother-in-law's faithful and well-regarded servant. In fact, he had already served Kleeborn's father.

As the ladies approached, a young man passed by and greeted them courteously. It appeared as though he had been engaged up until then in a lively discussion with Herr. Müller.

Oddly, the aunt appeared to be attracted by the expression on the young man's face and visibly agitated, she continued to look in his direction for a few moments. As she walked up the steps leading to the house, she looked paler than usual.

Concerned, Herr Müller thought that a sudden illness had seized her and rushed forward to guide her toward the reception room situated beside the office. The aunt sat down immediately and explained that she was quite alright but that she had grown unaccustomed to the fresh air, having spent so many hours in the sick room with Victorine, and the strong sunshine and brisk air had been too sudden a change for her.

With relief, Angelika walked up to check in on Victorine. Meanwhile, the aunt stayed downstairs to speak with Herr Müller for a little while.

"Who was that young man?" asked the aunt eagerly as soon as Angelika had closed the door behind her. Herr Müller was thoughtful for a moment because at first he did not understand the question.

"Are you referring to the young Holm, who was just with me, Madam? Yes, he is quite a fine and considerate young gentleman. Since our Miss Victorine has been ill, he never fails to come to my office twice a day to inform himself regarding her condition. He always gets a more detailed report from me than from the servants. Well, thank God that today I was able to give him some very good news and he was certainly pleased to hear this."

"So, he is quite a close friend of the family, then? asked the aunt.

"Not exactly," replied Herr Müller. "Since the young gentleman has not established himself yet and is not of any prominent family, Madam. No one knew what to make of his late father who was neither doctor or lawyer. For a long time he lived with his only son outside of the city and no one knew him particularly well as he lived a rather secluded life. Well, dear Lord. This is an expensive area after all, and for someone who is not wealthy, it is best not to be too conspicuous."

"Did the father pass away recently?" asked the aunt with obvious interest.

"About three years ago now," answered Herr Müller. "Holm senior was actually quite a learned man and well-versed in mathematics and foreign languages. It's said that he had published a lexicon or something. Well, they say that the son takes after the father and he *did* apply his time at the university very conscientiously. Certainly this will equip him well for his present position. A merchant needs to be informed today and besides, it's quite in style these days to be educated or at least *look* educated."

"Then the young man was not originally groomed to become a merchant?" asked the aunt with increasing interest.

"Ah, what did he want?" answered the bookkeeper. "No, madam, the young Holm is a Doctor of Laws.[16] He has studied properly. As recently as a year and a half ago, he made a change in his career and oddly enough, no one had noticed that he had demonstrated even the slightest inclination in the merchant trade. He seemed to develop this interest quite suddenly, but as you can see, Madam, where there's a will, there's a way. Two years ago, young Holm did not know how to calculate an exchange rate, or how to properly issue change, and product knowledge was a complete mystery to him. And now, he is the right hand man at Fischer and Company. Just watch, Madam, he will make his mark in the world."

The aunt, sinking ever deeper into reflection, appeared not to have heard the last words of the amiable old gentleman. Noticing this, Herr Müller kept respectfully silent with his usual reverence for Anna von Falkenhayn. When she was herself again, awakening as if from a dream, she commented that the young Holm should take part in business matters here more often, since this seemed to interest him so much.

"He does come to the firm's counting-house[17] often since choosing this vocation," replied Herr Müller. "But he hasn't come directly into the house, as far as I know. Other than coming to a few concerts, as he does sing a wonderful tenor. It's quite natural that he asks about our *Fräulein* Victorine's health. After all, he knows her fairly well and half the city already enquires after her, too. Look, Madam, there lies the sheet where all enquiries just from this morning have been recorded. Two full sheets of entries, although only half of them are legible. What a disgrace. The servants' writing is almost indecipherable! But here are the more elegant signatures of some young gentlemen. Almost all of them have added to the list themselves because they usually come alone to enquire after *Fräulein* Victorine. Look, at these names, Madam. Sir Robert Beverley, John Simpson Esquire, Comte de Beauchamp, Graf Nordhausen, Baron Engeström, so many strangers on this list."

The discussion came to an end when Angelika's face framed with blond curls peered into the doorway. She had been concerned about the aunt's long absence.

Anna proceeded to Victorine's room and found her sitting on the sofa, besieged by a crowd of young girls all chattering simultaneously; Babet and Agathe among them. They seemed to be discussing quite interesting topics but the aunt could not follow the conversation all that well, so decided to sit in her easy-chair at the farthest corner of the room.

Her thoughts returned to the faded past of so many years ago. At this moment, though, the memories were unusually crystal clear. Sometimes the sun bewitches us with a single bright ray of light in the middle of winter, making us think of spring when in fact the flowers have long since shrivelled and disappeared.

Anna surrendered herself completely to this bittersweet dream and abandoned her quest for the moment. What brought these thoughts on? Why now? She reflected on this, ignoring what was being said in the circle of young girls, although she was close enough to hear every word.

The girls were talking about the balls that would be taking place in the upcoming weeks, and of course they had a lot to say about potential dancing partners.

"Oh it looks rather dubious," sighed Babet. "If only Heaven would send us a fresh supply!"

"Unfortunately this is the case," agreed Amelie, the daughter of their neighbour, the Colonel. "Theodor leaves tomorrow and even Baron Sillborn is travelling to Vienna."

"And Lieutenant Horsten only has two more weeks of holidays," interjected Lilli.

This penetrating discussion continued for some time and in fact was so absorbing that no one noticed Victorine until Angelika stepped into the room, and with a horrified cry alerted them that Victorine had sunk back in her pillow looking pale and rigid as death.

What a commotion followed! Blinded by fear, the girls ran desperately around the room, screaming at the top of their lungs.

The housekeeper stormed into the room. fortunately followed closely by the doctor who had immediately been called.

"Bon Dieu! Qu'est il donc arrivé à ma pauvre petite!" she cried.

Victorine's unconscious state, aggravated by the hysterical and disorganized approach used to help her alarmed even the aunt and it took some time before she was able regain her composure and take control over the chaotic situation.

The resolute doctor reprimanded the girls for their actions, and one by one they crept out of the room. He maintained that this noisy visit had been too strenuous for Victorine and once again recommended uninterrupted peace and quiet for his patient. Babet and Agathe were banned from the sick room and he frowned upon any future social visits. Only Angelika, with her quiet demeanour was permitted to help the aunt in caring for Victorine as before, because her beloved benefactress vouched for her behaviour.

It was late evening and the aunt was sitting by Victorine's bed. Suddenly Victorine rose from her agitated sleep, drew back the curtains and with nervous haste looked around the room.

"Aunt," she whispered apprehensively. "Aunt, are we alone. Can we have a little privacy?"

The aunt assured her that no one would disturb them and asked her to remain calm.

"Calm? Calm?" answered Victorine with unusual vehemence. "Why not ask the storm that is howling and raging around the house to be calm! Or the sea? Or a flame to consume its own rage!"

"Dear child," interrupted the aunt. "You will drive us all to the grave if you continue in this manner! Come, be a good girl and lie down again, be patient and I promise . . . "

"What?" cried Victorine. "What can you promise me for my life, Aunt? What can you promise for the rest of my life, for all my happiness here on earth and perhaps even beyond! You must listen to me. You must listen to me right this minute if you don't want to see me lose my mind. You must listen to me and you must help me, because you are the only sister of my dear departed mother! Great heavy tears flowed from Victorine's wide staring eyes, splashing over her glowing cheeks, falling to her trembling breast. The aunt held her, caressing her with tender words, gently warning her to think of her health.

"Of course I will help you in any way I can. I am here for you. You know that I have come here only because of you. But please try to relax now, so that you can get your strength back again. Later, tomorrow, maybe . . ."

"Later is too late!" cried Victorine with ever increasing fervour. "Later, when everything is over, what kind of consolation is that? How can you help me then, when God Himself cannot undo what has happened. No! Now! Right now!"

It was useless for the aunt to remind her about the doctor's instructions, that she should keep still and preserve her strength.

"That old know-it-all! No one understands! Don't you see, Aunt? Don't you see that I have my strength back? But to be quiet now will destroy me. I cannot just turn off this monstrous fear that is engulfing me. I will explode, I tell you. Please listen to me, if you want to save me from destruction."

Victorine's eyes blazed feverishly. She pleaded over and over again with ever increasing ardour. Finally, the aunt surrendered, believing that she was giving in, so that she could pacify Victorine. She would agree to listen, on one condition.

"So tell me, Victorine. Explain to me what I can do to soothe you? If anything can be done, I will do it. But if it is something that I do not need to know at this moment, then save it for a more appropriate time, when you are calm again, when you are stronger. So, I will risk disobeying doctor's orders. Now tell me, what's troubling you, Victorine."

"Well, then. You must request that old Müller come upstairs. I would like him to go the room next door and keep the door open. And don't whisper about with him. I must hear everything. Every word that you say to each other. I will not be deceived."

"What is it then, Victorine? What do you want to know?"

"Is he going to Odessa[18]? Oh God! Perhaps he has already left!" wailed Victorine.

The aunt was visibly shaken, because she now believed that her niece was delirious.

"Victorine, please come to your senses. Control yourself, my dear," she said reassuringly. "What is this about Odessa? What should our dear old Müller do there?"

"Who is talking about *him!*" replied Victorine crossly. "Raimund, dear Aunt! Raimund Holm is going to Odessa! Maybe he is already there. Didn't you hear? It seemed to be so loud! So terrible! It felt as if the ceiling had crashed down over me. And you didn't hear anything? Luzie talked about it when the girls were discussing their dance partners; *the best among them*, she had said, *Holm is leaving today or tomorrow for Odessa.*"

With a deep sadness, the aunt looked at the distressed girl with a wild fear in her eyes. Then she covered her face and whimpered plaintively. "He has left! He's gone! Gone forever!"

"Holm hasn't left," replied the aunt. Laboriously she tried to recover her usual serene composure. "I saw him briefly this morning. Before you fainted. He was asking Müller about your condition. That kind old gentleman talked with me for some time about Holm, his commendable qualities, as well as his prospects for the future. He said nothing about Odessa, and Müller would not have neglected to mention this. Maybe all this about Odessa is just a fabrication? After all, who would undertake such a journey at this time of year? Winter is just around the corner!"

Victorine suddenly sat up in her bed and looked very closely at her aunt. Then she grasped hold of her hands and pressed them to her wildly beating heart. Her eyes were glowing, her lips trembled as if she wanted to speak, but overcome with emotions, she could not utter a sound.

"Oh, sweet image of my sister," said the aunt, overpowered by love for her niece. I don't want you to come to me only for compassion and affection because I also want to speak truthfully to you. Poor, dear child! Relax now. I will also try to relax. We'll both try to gather strength, because we will need it."

"I know this, aunt." answered her niece less distraught than before, but still upset. "I know it. Perhaps you are still unaware but I know everything already. And I know why it was *you* that was requested to come and see me. I don't know you very well, dear Aunt, but I know more than I can say. But I feel compelled to look upon you as a second mother, and to love you. So am taking this risk. To ask you and to warn you. Please don't try to do what will be requested of you. And I will say this in advance. Certainly you and my father have the power to break my heart, but you cannot force me to betray this love that is true; this love that I am willing to make any sacrifice for. If you don't want to believe me, or if you refuse to fulfil my request, well then you should focus that wonderful persuasive power of yours to try and dominate the mind of someone else. I intend to remain steadfast in my belief. You should not tempt me or try to stifle my deepest convictions about justice and injustice."

Perplexed, the aunt did not say much to her niece who was still unnaturally upset but with gentle coaxing, she was gradually able to soothe her a little. Bit by bit Victorine's story unravelled. Her emotional outpourings over the next few days, occasionally interrupted by comments from her aunt are summarized for the reader in the next section.

CHAPTER 5

Raimund Holm was the son of a man to whom the world had frequently been unkind in his short life. Evidence of this was not only in the prematurely grey hair, and the expression of bitter grief on his face, but in the seclusion that he anxiously sought and the timidity with caused him to flea even the most distant threat of anything that could coax him out of his shelter back into the light.

Experience had taught him that it is easier to live undisturbed and go unnoticed in a large and crowded city than in small town or in the country. Every newcomer draws attention to himself in a small town or village and he is regarded as odd or eccentric if he behaves differently from those around him. For this reason, Raimund's father chose to live in a large well-known commercial town. There, he lived for over twenty years until his death, equally distant from poverty and affluence and isolated from friends and society.

Refined manners and habits and a certain elegance in his appearance were not so easily discarded, even in the deep seclusion he had chosen, for they had been acquired in his youth. Obviously, he had known and had received an education in the world from which he had retreated.

Early on, he routinely shared these assets with his son, thus giving him an adequate preparation for his future entrance into society. When these qualities are missing, the world is inhospitable and uncompromising, even when someone who has grown up in isolation is otherwise talented and excels in every other respect.

The father had brought his son to this retreat as a very young child and educating him in art and literature, the joy and treasure of his life, was the father's main preoccupation.

Among high-spirited playmates, Raimund grew up the happiest and most energetic of all, for his father did not want to deprive his son of any youthful amusements, often permitted him to visit the public school, in conjunction with his own home tutoring.

Even though he had chosen this limitation in the autumn of his own life, the father was not intending to prepare his son for a contemplative life, permanently distant from the world. Instead, he hoped to educate his son for useful and active membership in society.

As it is possible to appreciate the true pleasure of tranquillity only after accomplished work, the true value of solitude is only understood after extensive experience in the confusing hustle and bustle of the world. Raimund's father had learned this from experience.

Like a spring dream, the boy's childhood passed by and almost imperceptibly, the time came when he had to leave his father, so that he could attend university.

For this first excursion into the world, the young lad felt confident and strong, owing mainly to his early education at the side of a noble and high-principled father. Unknown and uncelebrated, the father nevertheless remained a constant presence, through instruction and by example. In fact, the boy would seek refuge in his father's picture whenever he needed help or advice with life's turmoil and confusion.

When entering society for the first time, it is probably not advantageous to refer to a name made famous through the father, as reputation is obstinately associated with it. And so the innocent son of a man who had been deemed to be unworthy now had to struggle to prove his own innocence and his own value against a thousand prejudices and vexations. Everywhere this discrimination confronted him, simply because of his father's disgraced name. There was another disadvantage to this name, too. People simply expected him to be better and more clever than his peers and this expectation made him feel somewhat insecure, something that would not have happened if he had been born with a different name.

Fortunately, Raimund was not affected by any of this. Having the benefit of his father's collected experience supporting him, Raimund left home a robust, energetic and eager young lad and at an appointed time, returned in the same spirit.

With a clear purpose in mind, he had used his university years well and the advice of his father had persuaded him to prepare for an active life. Before making an appearance in the business world, he prepared himself by quietly continuing with his studies and acquainting himself with society.

Drawing on the recommendations of his father, Raimund had the pleasure of meeting acquaintances in the city, visited various organizations, went to balls and the theatre, but every night with his usual love and loyalty he went home to his father So the young man strove to cheer up his ailing father with colourful stories of the bustle from the life that the old man had not seen for twenty-five years. Nevertheless from his son's descriptions, he recognized the landmarks of his past and realized that they had not changed all that much.

At first, it almost seemed as though Raimund's father was being rejuvenated living together with his son again and through their lively discussions, but sadly this was only an illusion. In actuality it was the last flickering of a dying flame. The pleasant cheerfulness was not enough to sustain a life crushed by the power of resentment and antagonism over so many years.

After his father's death, Raimund stood alone and forsaken at his grave.

His last year of education still remained to be completed but the loss of his father did not outwardly change his situation. Living moderately as he was accustomed to do, the inheritance from his father secured him if not a brilliant at least a fully independent existence.

Yet he felt the most painful desolation in his heart for he had no one to care for, no one left to please and no to whom he could confide his thoughts and feelings.

Just when he was ready to surrender to that wistful and vulnerable mood precipitated by a loss, such as the one he had suffered, the exceptionally beautiful Victorine appeared in his life.

The city's best-known music teacher had organized a singing group, based on Zelter's praiseworthy example. The group assembled a few times a week and everyone who was musically inclined was eager to participate.

The founder of the group had been familiar with Raimund's wonderful tenor voice for some time and his presence was essential, and Victorine rightly claimed an equally important position as first soprano among the ladies. It was quite natural that musical talent would bring the first tenor and first soprano closer together and there were numerous occasions where they were able to express their thoughts on topics other than music, and little by little they came to discover each other.

Before this time, Raimund had occasionally seen and admired Victorine but the prevailing mood at the Kleeborn house deterred the proud modest young man from approaching.

Even now, though he was better acquainted with Victorine, he still avoided situations that would make him appear forward, though he often daydreamed about her lovely youthful figure and her dark fiery eyes. After leaving the singing group, her pure clear voice would still echo for a long time deep in his heart.

Some time after the establishment of the singing club, a festive ball would offer Raimund the opportunity to see Victorine for the first time in her full glory.

When she entered the ballroom, he could hear soft whispers of admiration rushing towards her, paying the highest tribute to her beauty, just as the treetops in the forest softly stir when the sun rises. These murmurs of acclamation accompanied her as she walked through the room, along the long row of already assembled guests, who seemed to have already proclaimed her as the queen of the celebration.

Inevitably, Raimund was captivated and watched every movement she made. Never before had a woman appeared so dazzling, never had Victorine looked so bewitchingly beautiful to him. Her luxurious dress, with all its splendour was nevertheless a perfect reflection of artless simplicity. Girlish merriment shone in her eyes and the pretty smile on her exquisite mouth enhanced her beauty beyond words.

She stood there in the middle of the crowded room, surrounded by her admirers and laughing with some and joking with others, acting like someone too accustomed to such adoration to take it too seriously. All who were even slightly acquainted with her pressed closer.

The most elegant young men approached her deferentially, as if she were a princess, in order to ask her for a dance and everyone envied the lucky one to whom she granted this request. Even the other young ladies considered it an advantage to appear to be on familiar terms with Victorine and to compete against her would never have occurred to anyone. Everyone liked her because of her unpretentious ways and perennially friendly nature.

Observing the crowd around Victorine from a distance, Raimund felt a strange sadness but could not understand why he felt this way. He tried to rationalize his uneasiness as a kind of sympathy for this graceful woman. He believed that this deluge of pretenders would only bring ruin to her in the end, yet he could not deny her this tribute that was her due.

They began to dance and Victorine, like a goddess followed by her nymphs[19], floated on the arm of a foreign prince, who lead the dance in this group of guests.

Only one girl remained seated because no one had asked her to dance. No one seemed to know this unsophisticated girl, whose almost too austere, somewhat old-fashioned dress had been ridiculed by some because it contrasted too drastically with the elegance of the other young ladies.

Embarrassed, with glowing red cheeks, the abandoned girl now sat by herself. No one had spoken a word to her. Her innocent young eyes glowed with passionate yearning wanting so much to share in these youthful amusements. At the same time, her young mouth twitched with anxiety and embarrassment, as if the poor girl was desperately trying to force back tears that came from an overwhelming sense of rejection.

Raimund did not participate in the first dance, nor did he take part several ensuing dances. From the corner of the room he was able to follow Victorine's every move. To his astonishment, she approached the unfamiliar girl immediately after the first interval between dances and started a conversation with the obviously flustered girl. Victorine sat with her a while and then, taking her by the arm, they walked up and down the hallway. But in the commotion of the crowd he soon lost sight of them and already he was plagued by a cruel suspicion. Perhaps Victoria, very aware of her extraordinary beauty, was only playing a malicious game with her? Perhaps she was only using this rather plain and unassuming girl as a foil so that she could accentuate her own allure?

Suddenly he was awakened from these daydreams by a soft voice calling his name. Startled, he looked up to see Victorine standing in front of him with a gentle pleading expression in her eyes.

"I would like to ask you to perform an act of chivalry, if I may. You look as though you would not refuse me," she said with an enigmatic charm. She blushed a little but continued, "I would like to ask you if you would ask that young lady to dance the next dance with you. I am referring to the young lady who just walked along the hall with me. She is not known in this group and unfortunately our bad-mannered young men here allow her to perceive this."

Raimund's happy surprise with this unexpected request left him speechless at first. He hurried away to fulfill Victorine's wish and quickly came back to her to find out more about the young girl that she was looking after so seriously.

"I know her about as well as you do," was Victorine's simple answer. "However, she is a stranger here. And when I saw her sitting there so forlorn, I thought about how I would feel if something similar would happen to me. So of course it was impossible for me to rest until I saw her dance."

"But how could you ever entertain this possibility, Miss Victorine, that something similar could happen to you," asked Raimund.

"Why could this *not* happen to me?" replied Victorine. The old custom of greeting a stranger with courtesy is no longer unfashionable, though being a stranger is actually just a kind of temporary misfortune. It could very well happen to me if I ever find myself in a place where I am completely unknown. Then I would find myself completely isolated, just as this poor girl. I have just learned that she is being asked to dance by someone else. Now I can enjoy dancing much more because I am no longer tormented by the sad expression of this girl."

"A girl you hardly know?" asked Holm.

"A girl I hardly know. Must we *know* everyone?" answered Victorine with a smile as she leaped away with her dance partner, who had come just at this moment to ask her to dance.

When the dance was over, Victorine sat down to rest and Holm approached her again.

"I wish I could be in your shoes, Miss Victorine, if only for just one hour," he said pleasantly. "It's probably a foolish notion, but I cannot seem to suppress my desire to know. Where does a person find this self-possession, this ability to radiate a feeling of wonder and joy everywhere with every smile, and every expression?"

"You are being very childish," laughed Victorine heartily. Only princesses have that kind of awareness, someone who is indoctrinated with such foolish notions already at childhood. That type of thing would never occur to people like us."

"Miss Victorine, you are too modest. If I may, I would like to add: At this moment, you are not being quite fair to yourself. How can you escape this impression that you create by your mere appearance?"

"I am not half as modest as you might think," answered Victorine amiably. "I would have to be a silly fool, if I did not realize how much or in fact how little I would credit myself with what you refer to as admiration," she continued. "I know very well that I could be rather unpleasant and perhaps even somewhat nasty and society's attitude towards me would remain unchanged, as long as everything else stayed the same. Before being whisked away by her dance partner, she smiled pleasantly adding, "I tell myself this quite often, to avoid becoming haughty."

Stirred by an unexpected and unfamiliar feeling, Raimund watched her go. He had often applauded her beauty, her spirit and musical abilities, but the kindness, genuine modesty and candid simplicity which he had just discovered this evening, as she celebrating a triumph that would have made a thousand others light-headed almost propelled these qualities into the realm of the supernatural.

For the remainder of the evening, he stayed by Victorine's side. He asked her for a dance, which she courteously accepted immediately. With her, he floated through the ballroom as if carried by heavenly wings, feeling a bliss he had never known before. At the table, where only ladies sat down, and the young men served, he stood behind the chair claimed by this young lady.

Prompted by Victorine's example, he tried his best to comfort the other girl who was still being ignored by most people at the ball. Periodically, Victorine rewarded him with a smile or a few words directed at him from across the table. With a poise bordering on serenity, she accepted the homage paid by the young men. With the foreign prince in their midst, they crowded behind her chair, competing for her attention or for the privilege of occasionally bringing her a plate of food or a glass of water.

Dizzy with happiness, Raimund returned home from the ball. The night was over, but he was still soaring in an enchanting new world.

He saw Victoria again and again and she now treated him like an old acquaintance, as someone with whom she could be completely at ease. Every meeting, he explored the depths of this gentle and kind nature and every discovery offered him new proof of her bright vibrant spirit. Richly endowed and resourceful, she was always ready to accept everything good, superior and right.

But Raimund never witnessed the ferocity that overcame her when confronted by an unexpected contradiction; a perseverance bordering on obstinacy. Tenaciously she would hold on to what she had gained and heedlessly execute what she believed to be right and good. Certainly he never saw this because the opportunity was never presented.

In Victorine, Raimund experienced the essence of the delightful exhilaration of exuberant youth, alive and breathing in his presence, where only the unattainable dream of his young imagination had hovered before.

He felt that they were meant to be together. Without succumbing to vanity, he had to admit that after a few days, it seemed that Victorine had also singled him out above all others.

Her charming blush, her eyes that flashed with joy when he came near, the unusual tremor in her voice when she spoke to him and a thousand other little signals too tender to express all announced his good fortune before a word was spoken.

Though this blossoming youth was inevitable, its genesis, what Holm said, what Victorine answered was never revealed in detail to the aunt. Almost wordlessly, the happy couple understood each other, almost wordlessly they had signed an indissoluble covenant of loyalty.

Raimund felt as though he could now fulfil his highest dreams and decided that he would immediately set himself to acquiring the skills he would need to succeed in life, and then approach Victorine's father so that he could ask for her hand in marriage.

CHAPTER 6

Certainly Raimund knew about Kleeborn's aversion to allowing his daughter to marry anyone other than a merchant, as this was known throughout the city, but Victorine was convinced or at least tried to convince herself that this was merely a pretext used by her father in his attempt to remove aristocratic young men from the competition arena. Invariably, it seemed to Victorine, he would express this rigid dislike of aristocracy, and yet he would never mention the other social classes.

Raimund wanted to believe Victorine. What doesn't a hopeful love want to believe? In this free imperial city[20] where they lived, Raimund was on the way to achieving his place in society and he was confident that he would attain everything he aspired to because he could see no significant rivals challenging him for the same goal.

The goal that he was striving towards was still distant, but Raimund and Victorine were able to wait patiently for the day of their complete union and were so happy with the present, that they were not overly concerned about the future. After all, who is not secretly a little afraid of even slight changes in his condition, even when these changes lead to better things?

In any case, Raimund did not conceal from himself that his little bit of property could not compare with a prince's fortune, but his mind rose high above those who have notions of noble-minded poverty and consider money to be more important than love, making generous theatrical displays of self-denial, even at the expense of happiness . . . and anxiously calculated the fortune of the beloved.

What significance did wealth have? Victoria now belonged to him and she had offered herself freely. Raimund would not have loved her less if she had been poor and in his eyes, the fortune which she would inherit one day could not raise or diminish the value of her gift.

In any case, he felt that he had more than enough strength to not merely adequately protect the woman that he loved from hardship or want but to actually provide her with everything that is required for a life of comfort and respectability.

He was not concerned about how the world would judge him. In fact, if he had thought about this, he would have remembered his father's words. His father had taught him that he should not attach more value to society's opinions than what it deserved. Never should he define or restrict his future happiness according to someone else's single decisive judgement on his conduct.

While Raimund seriously pursued entry into the active life of a businessman, Victorine decided to help ease the way for him and to safeguard as much as possible their envisioned future.

Until now, no one knew about Victorine's feelings because she did not have a single confidant, an intimate friend who is just as essential to a young lady in the normal world as would be the case in French theatre.

Unlike so many other young ladies, who are tempted to elaborate or embellish real or imagined love stories, Victorine had never had the need to talk incessantly about her feelings or to write long letters so that she could shine like the heroine of a novel in the eyes of their friends.

On the other hand, to be so clandestine was against Victorine's honest forthcoming nature and therefore she decided to take the first opportunity to confess the hidden secret of her heart to her father and to plead her case and justify her love.

She did not have to wait very long for the favourable moment. Finding her father alone and in a happy mood, she approached him. Unfortunately, his reaction was not as she had anticipated.

"So you have read some novels, child and they have not agreed with you," replied Kleeborn as soon as he realized what she was talking about. His ironic composure stung her like the thrusting of a dagger.

"Don't worry, my dear, life goes on. You are still young and have a lot to learn," her father continued in the same tone of voice. "You will see in time that the world is very different from the way it is depicted in your books. In any case, you may realize sooner or later or not at all, so I emphasize that your father is not so foolish that he would allow his company, a company that is known throughout the world, to extinguish with his death. Or would he ever hand over his only child to some romantic hero who has no concept of how to manage or maintain a fortune that he has acquired with his own blood, sweat and tears!"

Victorine wanted to intervene here, but her father made this impossible.

"You can put these silly notions out of your mind, along with any other foolishness!" he cried with a fiery look in his eyes that immediately silenced the girl.

"And I warn you. Don't contradict me, because it won't help and I expect you to comply with my demands. I have made it perfectly clear that I will never accept a baron, count or prince as my son-in-law. Nor will I tolerate a scholar or intellectual. My son-in-law must be a man of my station, the best and most honourable station in the world because it is the most useful one. By the way, you forgot to give me the name of your Céladon.[21] Never mind, I don't need it, it doesn't matter to me what this arrogant fool is called. Now you know how I feel about this matter, so go and handle yourself accordingly."

The icy manner in which Kleeborn expressed this judgement and his complete indifference to Victorine's feelings as he waved her away, convinced her that any attempt to soften her authoritarian father would be futile. In any case, at this time it was impossible for her to remain in his presence, her trusting nature had been stunned by his unexpected reaction. With an indescribably painful shock she now learned about the seriousness of life, and how fate conceals thorns among the roses along the pathway of life, unsettling even those whom she favours.

Until now every desire, every fleeting self-indulgence had always been fulfilled. Nothing had ever been refused Victorine or withheld from her before, but now pain, anger and an anxiety over her future brought hot burning tears to her eyes. Until this moment, Victorine had only felt tears of joy or compassion.

This was the first time that she realized fully what Raimund meant to her. In fact, she discovered that she had never loved him as deeply as she did at this very moment. The thought of being separated from him had never entered her mind before.

Her tears dried when she convinced herself that she would confront this obstacle with all the strength of her love, and the uncompromising force of her determined fiery courage.

Without further thought, Victorine seized her pen and proceeded to write her beloved a frank and accurate account of what had taken place between her father and herself. Her words were etched with the glow of an unusual passion, ignited by a sense of injustice that was entirely new to her.

She gave little thought to choosing her words and the longer she wrote, the more determined she became. But she felt at last that her words were not forceful or expressive enough to convince her beloved of the loyalty and trust that was in her heart. Above all, she wanted to comfort him, to convey how confident she felt at this moment about their future happiness.

"I belong to you, Raimund," she concluded after relating all that had happened earlier. "I am yours and will remain yours even if you were across the ocean, even though other stars may illuminate your way in other corners of the world, even though far away from me, the sun is rising above you just as it is setting for me. Then midnight would be morning for me and I would dream away the day and live only for the night, if I knew that the light would make you happy and that you were thinking lovingly about your Victorine. Have faith in me, because nothing can turn you away from me, no appeals, no threats, no power of time, or lethal force."

"Oh, if only I could cast off these golden chains, these chains that I vehemently despise. If I could just live a quiet modest life with you. Perhaps you think that I refer too casually to deprivations and other concepts I know nothing about. But believe me, my dearest, I know what I am talking about. I know that as a spoiled child I often dismissed as expressions of poverty what others cherished as rare luxuries. I know that my upbringing is a burden and that to a certain extent, I must re-learn everything about life if I am to leave this path that I have been accustomed to since birth. I don't deny that there will be some sacrifice involved, even if it must be a formidable sacrifice but just think of the joy of going through life hand in hand with the one you love. To soar with you to the source of everything that is good, true and beautiful."

"I was not born to endure pain, I know this since today. I just discovered this and this thought has overwhelmed me, it has crushed me. Just as for every living creature, whatever is good in me can only thrive in happy sunshine and only with you can I find this happiness I need."

"But I must go. I must give up this lovely dream of what could have been, because I cannot leave my father without his consent, if I value you and our happiness. Our joy was so near and now it's so distant from us. I will obey my father, just as I always have, and though I am writing this with fierce and bitter tears, my mind is clear. I will anticipate and hurry to fulfil his every wish; I will interpret his slightest gesture as my command. I will do everything; suffer, surrender, deprive myself, only so that I may love you. But he cannot forbid me from loving you, just as he cannot forbid me from breathing. The hand that created and sustains my beating heart set the seeds of this love right from the beginning; my life is interwoven with yours, it won't let itself be torn away. Any attempt to do this is a sin. It would be like spiritual suicide. For this reason I am yours and for this reason I remain yours, near or far, it doesn't matter."

"My darling! Just as I was writing, I felt compassion and comfort. How could it be otherwise? I feel your presence, you are near me, even now. Raimund, we still have the present for now, and we will still see each other and be able to talk with each other, just like before. Our common sorrow unites us all the more intimately. My father has not forbidden me all association with you; in fact he does not even know the name of the man who has captured the heart of his daughter for all eternity. At first, he did not give me time to say your name and later he did not think it worth his trouble to ask. So casually he treated the heart, the future happiness of his child! Yet even here there is a consolation. Well, I cannot blame my father for being cruel, since he does not know what this is doing to me. Perhaps he would have been gentler, for he has always loved me."

This was the first letter that Victorine had ever written to Raimund and she sent it to him concealed in a package of sheet music. This would not arouse suspicion since the singing association often involved such exchanges between members.

CHAPTER 7

There was no reason to doubt that Raimund had received the letter, but many days passed before she received a reply. Victorine's hopes of meeting him were impossible. He was nowhere to be seen. Not at the singing club or on the promenade, or at the concert or theatre. Not even a distant greeting.

A thousand ever-increasing anxieties and terrifying premonitions flooded her imagination. Try as she might, she could not escape this dreadful apprehension. She hardly had the strength to say Raimund's name, let alone dare to ask her acquaintances about where he might be.

Finally, after many days of overwhelming anguish, Victorine received a package of sheet music. With trembling hands, she opened the package that she had been yearning for. Raimund wrote:

"My dear Victorine! You, a soul so true and beautiful, who desires only to surrender all for love, to be happy with me. I am the lucky one. Duty permits me what is forbidden you. Yes, in sacred trust I have yielded all to you, all my previous hopes and dreams. I have given up at least for a while even my independence, only to be able to hope that I may win your hand one day. For the last two days I have been working at the office of Fischer's. His son, as you know, is one of my university friends."

"You are turning pale and your lovely eyes are filling with tears as you try to control your fearful anxiety as you read this letter. Take courage, dear Victorine. Don't worry and do not doubt me, because the step that I have taken was well thought out beforehand. I avoided seeing you these last days because I wanted to struggle with this battle by myself in quiet seclusion and I didn't want to write you until I had everything settled in my mind first. So that I could say: *I have done this rather than I am thinking of doing this.* I am just as outspoken as you are and I will always be this way with you, so I will not conceal this from you; that even I found it painful to tear myself away from everything familiar and from the path that my father had chosen for me, so that I could throw myself into the confusion and turmoil of a world that was never my own. But believe me: I will never regret a choice that I made only after considerable reflection and certainly from now on I will do my best to fulfil the duties and obligations of this worthy position which I have chosen for myself. A position I had to choose for myself, to be fair to myself."

"Dear Victorine, I have tested myself severely during this time and I have been very critical with myself, which is difficult since there is nothing easier than deceiving yourself. But I don't want to deceive you either, so I confess that I now know that I could live without you, but I also know that it would be like going on a winter journey every night, without warmth or light. For you are the sunshine of my life, without you I would be powerless, simply dragging myself through the darkness. So do not scold me for what I have done and do not envy me for being able to do what you are not permitted to do. And above all, do not blame your father for his well-intentioned motives, because if you look at these in the right light, he made it possible for me to show, with more than mere words, you what you mean to me."

"I hope that you feel better, to know that I already realize that I can begin this position, using already acquired knowledge that was intended for another profession. All that is missing is a little acclimatization and particular technical adaptation, something that boys usually learn early on. For the most part, this is not difficult to master and I may be spared some of this in any case. What is a heavy burden to a boy is an easy game to a man. Even if it is otherwise, how can I consider it a burden when I look forward to the goal I am striving for?"

A melancholic joy overwhelmed Victoria as she read this letter. The sacrifice that Raimund had offered did not fill her with love or admiration, but a nebulous nameless feeling drawn from both spheres and it intertwined her being with his. Only death would separate her from him now.

The two lovers would meet again. Their first reunion would be an achingly beautiful moment. From then on, there would be only fleeting glimpses or a hurried exchange of words, because both felt that more than ever now, they had to hide their secret from the curious eyes of society. For this reason, they conscientiously avoided any display of conduct that would have betrayed the sanctuary of their hearts to unenlightened observers.

CHAPTER 8

Over a year passed by in the bliss of the purest love and trust. Young Holm's hastily made decision was unprecedented for someone his age, with his knowledge and with his prospects for a very respectable position that was open to him and caused some sensation in this large city.

There was a lot of derisive talk at the beginning, as if he had committed some great foolishness, but later Raimund was making himself noticeable for an entirely different reason. People were compelled to admire the ease with which the newcomer, who was uninitiated in the ways of the mercantile class, was able to overcome difficulties, seemingly insurmountable problems even for those who had been brought up with the advantages of that class. Raimund's vast knowledge of foreign languages, the skill with which he managed critical business correspondence, and above all, his keen insight and evaluation of business ventures which he had turned into advantageous speculations, won him respect at the stock exchange.

It was known that he was working without remuneration at the office of the Fisher's, but the most prestigious businesses would have been glad to have such an assistant; one who worked like a seasoned professional though he hadn't yet survived his apprenticeship years.

If fate would reward his hard work and knowledge, he would be highly esteemed in the business world, they predicted. *Herr* Kleeborn himself mentioned Raimund several times in conversation over dinner. Victorine hardly trusted herself to lift her eyes over her plate. She felt as though her wildly beating heart would burst with joy, when her father's smiled mischievously as he emphasized Raimund's name. It seemed that he was betraying not only knowledge of her secret but his own special plans for her future happiness.

It was not unusual for him to summon her to her office, and so she followed him there, completely at ease and unsuspecting. At the most she expected to hear of a rejected marriage proposal and for this reason, so she was a little startled when Kleeborn approached her with an odd festive look, taking her hand and motioning her to sit down on the sofa.

"Victorine," he began after a little pause. Perhaps he had rehearsed his speech beforehand.

"Victorine, you are my only child and you know that it has always been my greatest wish to provide you with happiness, to the best of my ability. For many years, I have worked day and night to care and provide for you. Now it is your turn, to reward me for my care and effort. I must admit, to your credit, that you were an obedient child and you never had the slightest objection when I dismissed proposals that I considered inappropriate for you, since I didn't want to use my hard-earned money to rejuvenate old titles to nobility or redeem debt-ridden property. Well! A father's dedication builds a home for his children and my commitment has built a home for you. The reason I called for you was to announce that you will finally be a bride to a worthy man. A man of my class. A merchant after my own heart, he is . . ."

"*Herr* Holm is in the office," someone called into the door.

"*Herr* Holm," repeated Kleeborn absentmindedly, while Victorine trembled frantically.

He reflected a moment. "Well, that's good! Perhaps even better," added Kleeborn in a low voice. Then he turned to Victorine:

"As you know, business comes first, child. But stay here. This won't take long and we'll continue our conversation afterwards.

"Send the young man in," said Kleeborn to the clerk who had announced him. He left immediately to carry out this order. A few seconds later, Raimund appeared in front of Victorine. His first glance was for her. He saw that she was paralysed with bewilderment and his face turned red in his confusion.

Yet he quickly regained his composure and communicated his message to *Herr* Kleeborn with the utmost clarity. To be sure, he sounded a little hesitant at first but by and by his voice grew stronger. The topic was a certain business plan drawn up by Holms, which would be executed during a meeting between Herr Kleeborn and Herr Fischer.

Kleeborn discussed the negotiations in detail, and repeatedly praised the young man's intuition and clear perception. His manner towards Raimund was so friendly and polite that Victorine not only gradually recovered from her shock but actually began to entertain bold hopes about her situation.

The subject of conversation now exhausted, Holm was about to leave, but Kleeborn held him back.

"Before you go, *Herr* Holm," he said. "I want to demonstrate my esteem for you. I want you to be the first to congratulate my daughter on her engagement to Sir Charles Wissmann. Her future husband is the Dutch Ambassador in London and son of the owner of a famous company in Amsterdam, certainly known to you. For over ten years, I have been indebted to this company and this is the only way I can pay back my obligations to some extent."

Stunned by this unexpected revelation, Raimund turned pale and motionless as a marble statue. Thunderstruck herself, Victorine's folded hands trembled as she stared ahead with wide open eyes. She jumped up from the sofa.

"Father!" she cried. "Father, is this some sort of a cruel joke?" Her voice failed, silenced by inner anxiety that overwhelmed her. She was visibly shaken.

"A joke, my child?" repeated Kleeborn with a composure that seemed artificial. "Surely not! Since when do you know this jocular side of me? You should know by now that I don't joke about serious matters. Just ask Herr Holm here, he is certainly quite familiar with the company of your future father-in-law."

"It's not a joke, father? cried Victorine. In her distress, her self-possession was forgotten. "You aren't joking? And this terrible mockery! Father! I didn't try to hide anything from you. You know my heart."

"The hearts of young girls are articles of fashion. No serious, respectable man is taken in by them," interrupted Kleeborn.

"Besides," he added. "I hope that your heart is not a rebellious but dutiful heart, as would be expected for a daughter of mine. I don't know anything about the confessions you claim to have made to me and I urge you to forget these as well."

"Oh father!" pleaded Victoria anxiously. "You knew about my love. Stop trying to frighten me in this way. I haven't concealed anything. Even if you had a reason why you did not want to hear the name of the man I love, you should have been able to guess from Raimund's unusual decision. Yes! You did guess this! Try to remember, Father. You assumed who it was!"

"I didn't assume anything," replied Kleeborn dispassionately. "I don't spend a lot of time working out riddles, but I am well aware that young girls waste a lot time on dreaming up love stories when they have outgrown dolls. Every age group needs its toys. But Victorine, I really expected that you had left this nonsense behind. If you haven't done so yet, I ask that you do so as of today."

Pale and heaving with humiliation and a violent internal struggle, Victorine remained silent, while her father with a formal politeness turned to Raimund.

"Herr Holm! I have too high an opinion of you to believe that you would think that your present position or current financial situation would permit you to make claims on my daughter."

Raimund was about to respond to Kleeborn's words, but the older man would not let him speak.

"By no means do I want to discredit you, Herr Holm," he continued politely. "On the contrary, I know you as a trustworthy and talented young man, someone who will certainly make a place for himself in this world. Many have started life with less than you have and are millionaires today. If I can be of service to you at any time in the future, I will gladly do so because I enjoy helping young people find their success. But for now, as you well know, the future is not today and it's the fruit that gets picked and not the blossom."

In the meantime, Raimund had gradually regained his composure. The longer that Kleeborn spoke, the more Raimund was able to rise above his embarrassment and paralysed intimidation. Finally, with an almost regal composure he was able stand squarely before his opponent and look him straight in the eye, so that Kleeborn was now the embarrassed one and involuntarily turned his face away.

"I know who I am and I know what I am and I don't need a reminder from you, Herr Kleeborn to keep me within my proper boundaries," answered Raimund in a moderate, yet firm and serious tone of voice. "Yes, I admit it," he continued. "And I am proud to proclaim to you and the world that I love Victorine more than I love myself, more than good fortune, more than my life. But understand this. I love only Victorine and want to have *her*; and not the wealth of her father. I don't need it to make me happy, thank God."

"I let you speak, please extend the same courtesy to me," added Raimund as he noticed that the older man wanted to say something to him.

"You must have been aware," continued Raimund. "If I had stayed on the course for which I had been educated, most certainly I would have been able to offer your daughter a comfortable, and most assuredly a respectable and independent life. But I left that path, so that I could pursue the highest goals of my dreams, goals that you also admire. With time, I believed that I could be useful to you. I wanted to prove to her father that I loved his daughter with a rather significant sacrifice, as well as promise him an easy and carefree future some day . . ."

"Really? Well, that is very considerate and commendable," remarked Kleeborn, who still felt a little embarrassed. The upright and refined manners of the young man rather impressed him, and with regard to what had just been said and certain business considerations, he was prompted to handle Raimund with prudence.

"Yes," he continued in a friendly manner. "As I was saying, that is really quite considerate and commendable. And certainly you will thank me one day that I was so to speak the innocent trigger that set you on the right path again. You were born to be a merchant. And as I have stated, if I cannot accept your offer to my daughter at this time, I will always be available should you require my advice or any other service I can provide. For we shall always remain good friends and I depend on your honesty and trust that you will not undertake anything behind my back or seduce my only child into disobedience.

Before answering Kleeborn, Holm turned to Victorine. She looked as if she was at death's door, gasping in vain for air.

"My darling. My precious Victorine," he said and pressed her hand on his fiercely beating heart. "Victorine, you are my light, my life. Do not be angry with me. I must release you. I wanted to earn the right to your love, but not surreptitiously, not with deceit. Decide for yourself. And if it is your choice, then follow your father's will. Don't let my future fate influence your decision. Your happiness is my happiness. No one can take your image away from me. There is no real future for a heart that can only live in the past. I will always be yours, I can't do anything else, but you . . ."

"Raimund! Raimund!" cried Victorine, throwing herself into his arms and clutched his neck with a stormy fearful intensity. Then she sank before her father grasping his knees in desperation.

"Father," she pleaded. "Can you look upon me, your only child and not have pity? Can you listen to this most decent, honourable man and not welcome him and thank God that he wants to be your son!"

"Romantic heroine! Comedienne! You are wasting your time with these theatrical antics," stormed her father, blanched with fury and lips twitching with agitation as he tore himself away from Victorine's grip.

"Now get up! Dear God, this is going too far now! Get up, Victorine! Get up! You are and will remain the bride of Charles Wissmann, because I have given my word and I do not intend to break my word for the first time in my life because of your foolishness. As for you, young man . . ."

"Don't finish what you were about to say! Listen to my explanation first," said Raimund with a straightforward conviction that Kleeborn felt obliged to let him continue.

"After this, you can trust that I don't want to prevail upon you any further, and I repeat once more that I don't want to attain my happiness through devious means."

"And henceforth you will not secretly try to meet with my daughter? You will not write her? In other words, you are giving up all claims on her?"

"I don't have any claims on her, other than on her heart and only Victorine's decision is important here," replied Raimund.

"I am you . . . you are me," exclaimed Victorine emphatically and embraced him once more.

"Let me go, father!" She demanded with wild blazing eyes as her father tried to tear her away from Raimund. Shocked by the violence of her strength, he retreated.

"Listen to me, God. Listen to the vow I am about to make in the presence of my father," cried Victorine as she raised her right hand as if taking an oath.

"By my honour, I pledge my unswerving loyalty to this man. Nothing can every tear him away from my heart and nothing can move me to give my hand to any other man. And now, goodbye." Her voice softened as she turned to Raimund.

"Goodbye, my love, my youth, my only happiness on this earth. Raimund, I am yours and will always be yours. Promise whatever you want; I will keep my promise because you are my soul, my ideal, my everything! You don't want to have me accused me of perjury," she whispered in a broken voice and sank in his arms as if extinguished.

"Victorine! Oh my dear Victorine!" sighed Raimund. Tears glistened in his eyes as he let her slip gently from his arms to the sofa. He held her hand tightly in his own as he turned to her father, who was seething with a barely controlled rage.

"You have heard your daughter's words," said Raimund with respectful civility. "Victorine has requested that I act for the both of us. So, accept our promise then. We promise, on our honour, that we will neither try to see each other, nor write to each other, for as long as you forbid us to do so. I hope that your treatment of Victorine will not require me to rush to her aid. What more do you want?"

"I want you to separate," shouted, almost unintelligible with fury.

"We are separating, until fate unites us again. Here or there! said Raimund. "Calm down, sir. Neither of us is capable of deceiving you," he added firmly but with a sadness in his bright eyes.

Then he kissed Victorine's lifeless hand. "Goodbye, goodbye for a long . . . long time," he cried out. Then he left the room.

CHAPTER 9

"And nothing has changed, Aunt," said Victorine after recounting her story.

"We have kept our word. We do not see each other. We don't write to each other. But the air that circulates around me brings me greetings from him and the stars in the heavens light our way. They reveal to me that he is thinking of me and they reflect his image; surely my father cannot prevent this? No, his power does not extend that far. Nor can he force me to give my hand to a man I find loathsome and thus force me to commit the sin of perjury. Dear Aunt, please tell him this. Use your power of persuasion to convince him, so that he will cease forcing me to appear rebellious and disloyal . . . I am only doing what I must! Have sympathy and take us under your protection," pleaded Victorine with childlike innocence.

"Do you really think that you would have to solicit me to do everything in my power to do what is best for you?" replied the aunt gently. Certainly we must first determine what is actually the best for you and to support you, so that you can gain back strength enough to withstand confrontations that will sooner or later threaten you."

"Aunt! Dear Aunt," responded Victorine. "I am by nature not very forceful. With Raimund, I was always soft and quiet and docile as a child. But this now, means more to me than my own life! Of course, if the fates allow, one day the time will come when Raimund and I will be united. We can only be whole, with the other. We can only be complete, all that we can become if we are joined to each other. Take him from me and you rob me not only of all my happiness on earth, but also take from me any sense of justice or virtue. Without him, I am nothing! Oh God," she exclaimed with an infinitely painful gesture.

"Oh God! My poor insignificant being is being destroyed by crushing this generous beautiful heart. Who could forgive this murder?" she cried, her eyes streaming with tears as she hid her face.

Just at this moment, Angelika came in but noticing these two, she immediately turned around. She did not want to disturb them with her presence. The aunt followed her with her eyes.

"And how would you explain this gentle, loving apparition, Victorine?" she finally asked.

"Do you consider your pain equal to hers? Doesn't she have a life too? Do you notice that she now smiles sometimes? Haven't you seen the transformation . . . the tender buds bursting with new life? Oh, dear child, happiness and unhappiness are temporary. It is only the fulfilment of obligation and duty that makes our lives complete. Courage comes to us somehow; we don't know from where it comes, although we have a notion. The best among us transcend this pain, transform it and refine it instead of suppressing it."

"Aunt, for Heaven's sake, do you call Angelika's poor existence *life*? Are the buds of new life, as you refer to it, something other than never-blooming buds that want to weave themselves into a funeral wreath? What can you mean by this? Have you never lived? Never loved?"

"Well, perhaps!" replied the aunt with a whisper and ended the conversation for the evening.

To the astonishment of her friends, Victorine recovered unbelievably quickly from the last blow on her health.

The doctor got credit for this miracle but in fact it was the aunt who was responsible for restoring her, partially because through Herr Müller, she had been able to soothe Victorine with the news that Raimund's journey to Odessa had never been seriously discussed. The aunt had also relieved Victorine from the tremendous pressure of imposed silence by giving her permission to reveal the fears and passions of her troubled heart.

CHAPTER 10

In her happy youth, Victorine had not needed a confidant, consequently she had not been able to find one now that she needed one. But fate had been kind to her and provided her with the means to deal with her pain alone. It was actually the repression of her feelings that had brought her to the brink of death.

Now she found in her aunt, an empathy that could never have been possible with the good, though somewhat narrow-minded Virnot, or with her friends. Her aunt was an intelligent and responsive friend and though she was far from approving Victorine's behaviour, and in fact mentioned this with penetrating seriousness, she still listened to her with serenity and patience. This was a great relief for a passionate spirit.

Besides, the very presence of the aunt created a kind of magnetic force and that was quite wonderful and extraordinary. Her aunt never contradicted Victorine, she seldom asked questions; she simply listened to her.

Yet the deeply perceptive look of her clear eyes inspired Victorine with a new confidence. To the perceived opposition that she imagined in her friend's expression, she vigorously responded with her most intimate thoughts and buried emotions. With a confidence extorted almost invisibly, Victorine learned to unravel the mysteries of her own heart. For the first time in her life, wordless introspection was transformed to recognition and awareness.

Gradually life in the Kleeborn household returned to normal and the master of this household looked forward to the day when its massive halls would resonate again with luxurious splendour and the exciting whirl of society.

Every evening at a designated hour, he came to the living room, where the aunt with her usual merriment and gracious manners would preside at the tea table, sometimes surrounded by a few trusted friends. With satisfaction, he observed how the bloom of health was gradually returning to Victorine's pale cheeks and how her melancholic eyes were radiating with new light.

"Well, well," he said to himself. "Just as I thought. With time, everything will be back to normal."

Cheerfully, Kleeborn hurried back to the gaming tables where his friends were waiting for him.

One evening, when Victorine was feeling remarkably well, Kleeborn spoke with her before leaving. He talked at length about an elegant party where he planned to celebrate the his daughter's complete recovery.

Agathe and Babet, following Aunt's instructions, were working industriously on some new ball finery. The atmosphere was filled with waltzes, violin-playing and the girls envisioned little petticoats under flowery dresses swaying gently to the music.

Meanwhile, Angelika bustled to and fro and approached everyone, especially Aunt, asking how she could be of assistance. Angelika was enraptured and the silent pain of this gentle spirit gradually faded. She was becoming more sociable.

Everyone, even Herr Kleeborn felt drawn towards the warmth and generosity radiated by Angelika and felt obliged as far as was possible, to replace the loss she had experienced by being twice as kind in return. The quiet friendly girl naturally accepted this affection and comforting power with gratitude and found a new joy in life, though not in her own.

Angelika had the sensation of observing the life of a stranger; as if she were no longer a part of her own life. Only the pain or joy of others connected her to any earthly existence and for this reason it was her dearest wish to see Victorine cheerful and happy again. She felt that Victorine, whose life was so full, knew nothing about pain and loss.

Every evening, after Herr Kleeborn had gone, the aunt reached for a book so that she could read to the young girls. Her delightful voice was rich and resonant and she was a master of the art of reading.

From among the most eminent poets of our time, she based her selection on how well the poem could lift the minds of her two favourite girls and demonstrate to them how personal pain can be transformed in the light of poetry. In this way she opened the hearts of the young girls to the inspiration of poetry, showing how art rises far above earthly fate and teaches all of us with unaffected patience to overcome it by creating a private world that no power on earth can ever extinguish.

Agathe and Babet waited impatiently for the moment when the aunt would tire of reading and put the book down again, so that they could rush to their room and compensate themselves for the enforced silence during the arduous reading. Angelika, on the other hand, responded to the aunt's request and went to get her harp. With her sweet low voice, she strummed the golden strings and sang the following song.

Angelika's Song

When bright morning lights dazzle my eyes

I escape love's radiance

timid with myriad colours

Locked deep within my heart.

Unseen he rests, he glows hidden

Until the evening comes

The day is his.

Then, when gray shadows

Slowly turn light into darkness

Until the last ray dims

And night surrounds an endless sky

From deep within my heart

 I gently light the silent candles of love.

From a glorious past

They comfort my solitude with light.

Even in darkness they

Show the light of hope

And promises to come.

When tired eyes close to sleep

Like a beacon they glow

In the wonderful harbour of dreams.

Let these dreams blossom

As long as the dream surrounds me;

Let them follow me faithfully

Until I am put to rest

For my eternal sleep.

No. These flames will never die;

They light the way eternally.

When the song ended, tears glistened in the eyes of the audience, but the eyes of the singer remained clear. Her face was serene, as she stood up and silently carried out her harp again.

As soon as she had left the room, Victorine, overcome with emotion, ran to Anna's arms.

"Aunt! Please believe me when I say how much I understand this quiet lesson that you tried to teach me through this almost perfect angel, but can the young fir bend and wind itself like ivy? Dear, kind Aunt! I suffer with her when I imagine her future as mine. And I see how you want to raise me to Angelika's level, exceptional in her humility, but this will only bring me to an early grave!"

Her eyes overflowing with tears, Victorine buried her face in the arms of her aunt, who gently coaxed her to stand up again.

"My dear Victorine," she said. "My dear child, don't think that I don't know how everyone experiences pain and joy differently. How could it be otherwise for different natures? Do you really believe that I would be so unfair to expect everything from everyone? We all have different kinds of strength and we measure strength differently. But we do not recognize this strength or how far our courage extends until we have been tested. Though it really shouldn't, it always hurts and sometimes even makes me angry to hear: *I can't do this; this is impossible for me.* Oh we can do a thousand times more than what our cowardly inertia leads us to believe, if we truly want something. I am speaking from experience, my dear child. Or do you really think because I am old I never felt young, never experienced sadness the way you or Angelika have?"

"Oh Aunt! I believe you," replied Victorine with a sigh.

"But times were different when you were young. Times were better than they are now. A completely different world, even for girls! With all these procedures and requirements we have. I can imagine that even you may have felt as we do, but I cannot believe that you have experienced pain as deeply. In your time, there was peace and order, but we have a turbulent sea to deal with. Brazenly, the high surf carries us to port, or shatters our hopes; bringing us to our doom at the next cliff. Our ships only play in the whirlwind of time, every movement is a struggle."

"Certainly systems may have changed considerably since I was young," replied the aunt. "But principles never change and it is a childish though widespread belief that the world should change just because we have made our entry."

Victorine reddened but remained silent. Angelika entered the room and the aunt reached for her hand and continued to speak.

"Children, I don't generally speak a lot about myself, but I love both of you as a mother would and I have seriously thought over whether it might be appropriate to tell you of my own youth. I think, Angelika, that maybe you will find a new strength in my example. Perhaps you will see that you do not have a monopoly on suffering but that it is possible to suffer and still live on. And you, dear Victorine, maybe you will learn that the love in your heart is not necessarily the ultimate masterpiece, or the axis around which the world must turn and that what you call your misfortune is not a kind of nobility that sets you apart from other people. We are all born to love, to suffer and in the end to find our true happiness in sincere devotion. I think I will devote the first quiet evening when we three can be together to this rather serious topic, even though reliving some of those very sorrowful days may cause me a little pain."

CHAPTER 11

"Listen, Babet," said Agathe to her sister as they were getting ready to undress for the evening. "How do you feel towards Angelika?"

"Oh, don't ask! She's so dull and faint-hearted," answered Babet disagreeably.

"That's true, she doesn't really have much of a life," Agathe replied with a shrug. "But we should still be nice to her. Look, how much she helped me with my sewing, while we were listening to Aunt's lecture."

"Aunt certainly has good taste," added Agathe after a little pause while she closely examined the new dress. "And she really isn't half-bad as we first thought. Just think, she knows all about me and the Lieutenant, and the odd thing is, I told her most of this myself! I still don't understand how I came to do this."

"Really? And what did she say?" asked Babet a little dejectedly. For the thirtieth time she read fair-haired Theordor's farewell card, which she had secretly taken from the living-room mirror a little while ago.

"Oh, it was quite strange really" answered Agathe. She laughed a little. "Now this little heart isn't so important for the moment. That will be taken care of by the dozen pretty blonds and brunettes. Wasn't that a little frivolous, coming from such an old person? But afterwards she suddenly became quite serious and gave me all sorts of advice how I should behave towards *the dark-haired one*."

"So she finally scolded you," murmured Babet to herself.

"Scolded? Oh no, not really. Only a little bit," answered Agathe. "And you won't believe it, but it's true. She promised me herself, that he would be invited to the first party that we give. This is quite proper, since he has already visited Uncle. I saw the calling card myself. He will be permitted to lead me to the table and to sit beside me, but I had to promise to tell her everything that goes on between us."

"And you promised this?" asked Babet.

"Not exactly," replied Agathe. I naturally told her that it would be impossible for me to repeat every single word that is said between us. But she was satisfied with this. She laughed merrily and said that she was not demanding to know every detail, but that I should above all not intentionally conceal anything from her, especially those things that I would not like to tell her. Finally I promised her this and I think this might be useful to me, since she means well. I am even glad to have someone quite reasonable with whom I can discuss things and someone who can give me good advice."

"Oh, you foolish child! What fun is left for you then?" sighed the grieving Babet, who went sorrowfully to sit in a corner with her card. She thought of Theodor and the bliss of the last dance and cried wistfully until finally, overcome with grief, she fell asleep.

A few days later, a new famous opera was to be performed and Babet and Agathe were given permission to attend, chaperoned by *Mamsell* Virnot. Since Victorine's illness, they had been deprived of this entertainment and were now eager to go. So the quiet private evening was made available for the aunt's life story, as she had promised.

For several minutes, there was an almost reverent stillness in the room. Neither Angelika, nor Victorine wanted to disturb the silence. The Aunt looked so dignified and pensive as she sat down in her chair without speaking a word. Both girls remained quiet, not daring to utter a word or hint with a glance that would remind her of a promise she had made. She had, after all confessed that it would be painful for her to tell this story.

But the aunt did not need a reminder. After a short interval, though visibly agitated, she began to speak.

"We want to make use of this quiet evening that we have. As I have promised. Still, I feel rather odd about this; probably because I am not used to speaking about myself."

"I always knew too much about the world," continued the aunt. For this reason, I never wished that the world should want to know much about me. Therefore, you are the first to whom I am about to reveal my life's history. My story will be quite long, because I have had a long life. Sometimes my life was bleak, sometimes it was painful and sometimes there was poverty." Overwhelmed by memory, the aunt commented on her own reflections, while staring ahead sorrowfully, as if she were looking for something vanishing in the nebulous twilight distance.

Angelika quietly drew closer while Victorine with her customary sensitivity looked at the aunt with sympathy and embraced her.

"Dear Aunt Anna, if it hurts you to . . ."

But the aunt gently resisted Victorine's gesture.

"I'm all right, I'll be fine." she assured them. "I love both of you like daughters and a mother's love does not recognize pain. And there is some gratification in being able to look back on a perilous path that has already been travelled and with the experience we have acquired through our own struggles, try to guide those who are just setting out on this path. The aunt smiled though it seemed at first that her smile was forced a little.

"By the way, what I am about to relate is not an amusing fairy tale, which might better suit your adolescent taste, and yet it might seem full of fantasy when you look at the wilted figure of your old aunt and listen to her speak of a certain magic, the impact of which still has not died."

"That certain magic," repeated the aunt with fiery eloquence. "This magic that kept me young inside and maintained my strength in my older years. The magic that finally and brilliantly solved all the hieroglyphics of life for me. Although it came late, I learned to appreciate the wonderful gift of life. In pain and in joy, God had granted us love to accompany us through life. At the end of the day, and as gentle as the evening star before nightfall, the way to our resting place is lighted, until we are greeted again upon awakening."

Victorine and Angelika were deeply touched by the aunt. In their eyes, she appeared more lovely and youthful looking. An expression of peacefulness and lifted spirits after a long and difficult pilgrimage seemed to spread over her entire body. The girls hardly recognized their aunt. Perhaps, as before, a gentle spirit was taking another backward glance just before leaving earth and mankind behind to soar away to eternity.

"It's astonishing, how large and wide and powerful this chasm between then and now is becoming as I look back at my past," reflected the aunt a moment before continuing. "Indeed, it will actually be necessary for me to take a running start as everyone likes to do before taking a big leap forward. Certainly there is a gigantic distance between this hour now, to the time when I just turned fifteen. It probably seems strange and unbelievable to you that I was once that age," smiled the aunt. "But it's true. I really was once so young, even though it seems like a dream to me. It will be the same for you, children. Of course, by that time, the mound that covers my resting place will have already sunken down. Yes, that time will come and it will seem to you too, as if time hurried by too quickly for you. So let us not expect too much from time, it will catch up with us soon enough."

"Be still, children," said the aunt as both girls in simultaneous melancholic reaction grasped her hands and kissed them. "Be quiet, girls, and don't be so frightened by explicit images and sombre overtones that people of my age are only too happy to indulge in. You should not try to avoid them, at least not deliberately."

"And now I must ask you to interrupt me as little as possible while I am telling my story. I will start by describing our home life as well as our social life as it was over forty years ago, when I left the nursery and was introduced to a young girl's world."

"At that distant time, life for someone of your social standing was both richer and poorer. Poorer, much poorer in spontaneity and freedom; richer, much richer in the abundance and variety of amusements. Much richer too in pure enjoyment, because all that over-abundance that you boast about is in the final analysis quite exhausting. In fact, rarity has always been the best seasoning for pleasure."

"Do you think I am misleading you with this praise of my era? Perhaps you will at least acknowledge this other example; something that your grandmothers before you certainly appreciated. Hardly a trace of it remains of in our world today. I am referring to that special gallant attention, a regard almost bordering on a reverence reminiscent of chivalry. A courtly form of respect that women expected from all refined men. When we were in society, which compared to today, did not occur all that often, we entered the room like little princesses. We were surrounded by our attendants, who were anxious to please our every whim.

It is different for you, children. Men today appear to be on equal footing and believe therefore this expresses everything eloquently enough. You are to blame, for you have positioned yourselves beside them on slippery ground. Let me make an analogy so that I can better describe our relationship to young men those days. We were like flowers that were tended carefully in a locked conservatory. Access to this conservatory, where these beautiful flowers could be admired in closer proximity, was coveted. You, on the other hand, grow and bloom in freedom, and become perhaps more lush and beautiful. But you are in a bountiful garden accessible to the whole world, where anyone can approach you without restriction. Unfortunately, what can be seen on a daily basis loses the charm of novelty in the end. Before long, you become accustomed to them and walk by carelessly, and unfortunately many exquisite plants are neglected, or maybe even bruised and trampled in the confusion.

However, I will not deny that we probably would have envied the freedom you have today, if we had been able to vividly imagine such freedom. But such fantasizing would have been impossible, given our limited knowledge of the world, and those intimidating conventional restrictions. I must confess that we paid dearly for our genteel beauty with unimaginably painful high-heeled shoes, stiff whalebone skirts, and armour-like tightly-laced corsets.

In complete contrast to what us customary today, we were disguised to the point of being almost unrecognizable. Each of us was a constantly changing puzzle from the tips of our dainty sequined boots further enhanced with glittering jewel buckles, to the hairpins that decorated the tops of our towering coiffures. All day long, these monumental hair sculptures claimed our attention. Every draft, every rapid turning of the head threatened to topple these powdery pillars.

Those days, even the most attentive beau could not be certain of the hair colour of his fair lady because the yellow hair powder made blond hair identical to brown hair. With the help of high heels, short women were raised to medium height and whalebone stays ensured that all had the same impossibly tiny wasp-like waistline that disguised the true human form from any mortal eye.

You are laughing about the strange role we played. Well, I think I have would laugh too, if I could see myself again in all my finery! And yet, the beautiful young women among us did were not regarded as less beautiful and the plain ones were able to take advantage of this accepted camouflage, since these disguises allowed us to completely mask every flaw.

It is significant that in those days we all had time to accomplish any project for which we had accepted responsibility. I never heard the types of complaints so common today about not having enough time. The main reason that we had more time was simply because we stayed home more often than the younger generation of today. Morning visits or walks were not common and I would wager that there were not three times that my mother left the house in the morning in her entire life, other than when she went to church.

However, I don't want to extol the virtues on home-life too much because there was a certain stiffness and awkwardness in our customs too. Nothing caused us greater anxiety than having to present ourselves or our houses to our friends or acquaintances in a state that was less than immaculate. An unannounced visit where we would be forced to receive someone in a house dress or while we were occupied with domestic tasks, would cause just as much surprise as indignation. Only very important circumstances would excuse such an obvious social blunder.

So that we would not appear to be violating the strict rules of decency of our time, we were not able to go to the theatre, or walk on the Promenade unless accompanied by a gentleman companion and this made going out all the more complicated. Although this custom probably arose from the willingness of gentlemen to be of service to a lady, the gentlemen who would be considered appropriate for us were not always available or accommodating when we required this service. By the way, I am referring only to women; young girls did not step out into the street without the protection of their mothers.

Everything around us, whether animate or inanimate was governed by a certain formality that seems to be missing in our current less formal way of living. No one would ever think of leaning against one of our fragile finely-carved gilded *à quatre couleurs* chairs. The narrow matching *settees*[22] had nothing in common with the yet unknown sofas of today, other than as today, they also prompted a sort of pecking-order competition among the ladies. Incidentally, these *settees* offered absolutely no comfort and the reclining position that is so popular today was unheard of except in cases of illness.

In any case, it was impossible to lean backward in our outfits with our hooped skirts and colossal hairstyles. We sat very erect and I still do this out of habit without feeling any discomfort. This extremely correct posture however was closely associated with an exact observance of the accepted rules of etiquette among equals, even in close family circles, as well as a carefully calculated respect for one's superiors. Today this type of respect is dismissed as excessive, stiff and overly ceremonial but I cannot deny that occasionally I quite miss it.

Every day, before passing through the door, I greeted my parents with a dainty curtsey[23] that I had learned from my dance instructor. Before approaching, I offered each of them a solemn respectful *good morning*. I suppose that it would seem comical today, but we are creatures of habit and I think that when children approach adults with such reverence in the morning, they are unlikely to demonstrate extreme opposition or other bad behaviour later in the day, as seems to happen too often today.

The familiarity children use with regard to their parents today would have been considered blasphemous in my time. This intimacy would have only been tolerated with very young children. And yet mothers and fathers were not loved any less then than they are today. I loved and trusted my own parents so completely that I cannot believe that the prevailing tone of equality between parents and children could improve the relationship in any way. I must say that in some cases, and certain expressions, this equality is hurtful.

For many years, my father lived with the distinguished reputation and honour of a royal resident in the free city of N___. As the younger son of a very old family, where birthright applied, he was not rich. This was of significance, since my mother had not brought any substantial wealth into the family.

The income of my parents, in conjunction with my father's remuneration was only enough to permit us to live in frugal respectability. Certainly, fifty to sixty years ago, a family could manage with far less money. In those days, even the richest households of this city were dominated by a certain economical moderation, which perhaps we would dismiss as avarice or pettiness today. Thousands of luxurious inventions that are indispensable to us today were then yet completely unknown. We lived closely crowded together and required fewer services and did not have any costly fantasies to satisfy.

In spite of this, a certain elegance was important to us, whether in our attire or surroundings. At least twice a year our normally moderately set table would sigh and bend beneath the weight of heavy silverware, precious wines and the most exquisite dishes. So many guests, as many as our ballroom could hold, would sit at the table in all their finery, rigid with gold and valuable jewels, and all would be conscientiously and accurately seated by the master of the house according to rank and position.

At festivities such as these, the master and his wife always looked as though they wanted to rid themselves of a worthy though rather tedious duty as best as possible and even the guests wore expressions of polite resignation rather than pleasure. After all, a three hour dinner is an amusement few people really enjoy and in any case, these social events were never intended to be enjoyable.

No one expected anything different and on the whole these dinners were quiet affairs. The ladies observed everything, counting bowls and napkins and wondered how they would make arrangements at their own next banquet. The gentlemen ate and drank and towards the end of the meal let their wit shine with mischievous toasts to one another's health. However, when all was over, servants and guests thanked God at having once more weathered the occasion.

This is what social festivity was like in my day. Certainly my father had picked up a more pleasure-seeking and libertine attitude abroad, especially in France and yet he felt obliged to respect the customs of the city that had welcomed him so hospitably. Moreover, he was too sensible to swim against the stream, which in those days would have posed particular difficulties. The world then was far less tolerant towards eccentrics or to people constantly seeking new experiences. Today, there are reformers and instigators in every school and at every corner, propounding their grandiose ideas to a receptive and faithful audience. This expression, *Fool! You want to be more intelligent than we are!* That is how the uneducated brothers of Gellert[24] drove dancing bears from their midst and this tactic was in full force and quite normal in those days.

My father remained unperturbed and did not try in the least to alter the lifestyle of his friends and acquaintances. He consented to share in their celebrations but was guarded with the wealthy merchants among whom he lived, and avoided engaging himself in any activity that would disgrace himself or bring ruin to his family.

For this reason, he would select only a small number of guests to assemble at his properly set though modest table and my mother had the rare talent of being able to accomplish much with little and so we were able to repeat these little feasts frequently. This dear lady had such a sense of order and knew just how to use her carefully preserved items in the correct manner, so that even with modest means, our household was noted for a certain elegance that was not very widespread yet in this area.

Although our way of living was occasionally considered distinguished, we were forgiven, since it was obvious that we were outclassed in terms of wealth and grandeur. Our family was well liked because our parents were able to combine genuine goodwill and courtesy with attentive cordiality. This consideration teaches us to avoid anything that could potentially hurt even those of the lowest social status and to interpret everything as it was intended. My father had gained these qualities earlier in life with his dealings in the world, and my truly amiable and unassuming mother was born that way. And so, without ever having aspired to this honour, the two of them became the focal point of a fairly diverse social circle.

For twelve years, until the birth of your mother, dear Victorine, I was the only child of my parents and enjoyed the boundless fortune and misfortune this position involves. I was naturally endowed both physically and mentally with the happiest disposition and my parents had occupied themselves with the further development of these qualities. I must say that contrary to his nature, my father was rather extravagant when it came to awakening any latent talents I had.

So early in my youth, I made significant progress in music, drawing and painting of miniatures; all subjects that are considered essential for a young girl's education today. In fact, I exceeded the limits of accepted notions of female education of my time, but my little sphere was confined to a couple of sad Polonaise[25] tinkles, arduously copied embroidery patterns or at the most, painfully executed landscape watercolours modelled after certain copper-plates. My natural talent for learning foreign languages prompted my father and others to believe that tutoring English or Spanish would be a suitable career for me. In any case, we normally spoke French at home, as was customary in privileged families.

My father preferred this language to any other, because it allowed him to participate intellectually without having to devote himself to scholarly pursuits. Throughout his life, he favoured classical French writers and in fact these were the only novels he read. In his youth, he had learned little of the beautiful German literature and had not been encouraged by what he had read. That gloomy Gottsched[26] era offered little to a spirit such as his.

Therefore, my father retained an enduring prejudice towards all German writers, and especially German poets. This was a conviction he shared with almost all educated men who were actually following the example of King Frederick II[27]. Although I only learned much later to appreciate the literary treasures of my people, a brightly shining dawn had already made its entrance in the German art world around the time I was born, and enlightens us today.

Above all my other qualities, my father appreciated my excellent sense of perception, a quality that men only learn with great effort, but a natural ability for our sex. I was particularly insightful.

This peculiar gift to females would almost lead us to believe in good, or at least cheerful, fairies, who bestow on their favourite infants a magical power to comprehend at least all surface values at a glance. Without probing deeper into knowledge; or even desiring this knowledge, they flutter their gossamer wings lightly around its blossoms, and are happy to watch men sweat over the tedious work of digging out roots.

Not only do they delight to hear wise men speak because they comprehend so well, but sometimes with mocking audacity they dare to stand next to these sage men and confound them a little with their magic charm.

But this mental flexibility is not without danger for those who possess it. In my opinion, from my present perspective, it is better to put limitations on this ability, rather than to practice it or to be admired for it. And yet, my father had another view on this matter. He considered a modest and pleasing nature at home and in the world as the best qualities of my gender. He believed that in order to succeed, we required superior education but certainly not scholarship. According to my father, scholarship often proved to be more of a hindrance in life. He tended to smile with genuine pleasure at my little scientific pretensions and made allowances for me.

While my educational development amused and occupied my father, my dear flexible mother was encouraged by him to teach me as early as possible how to gain independence from those common routines that often keep the most talented women in oppressive subjugation. Through the years, my mother taught me and demonstrated how I could manage without seamstress or milliner. For emergencies, I also learned how to arrange my hair and to get along without a maid. No small matter in those days!

This was my father's way of mentally and physically preparing me for the future, whether it brought me to the wide world or to a secluded convent. Even then, I wore this religious cross; a gift from a noble godparent, where my grandmother had once been a lady-in-waiting[28] and it was no small reassurance to my father to know that I would be spared from the tribulations of life to some extent.

My parents nurtured me and I flourished under their care. I was as happy in my external world as in solitude, for I was never denied privacy. In those days, not every age, gender, or station considered reading essential, the way it is today. Those days, mothers sometimes had to admonish their daughters to finally take a book in their hands. Not like today, where exasperated mothers scold their daughters for their over-zealous reading dismissing it as nothing but busy idleness.

However, I began to read novels quite early in life. My father did not forbid it, especially since he did not believe in such restrictions. But he did monitor my reading selection and protected me from the French novels of that time, although he did not conceal that he preferred these writers, regardless of the corruptive tendency of their art.

Still, finding good reading material was more difficult those days. Worthwhile German novels were as rare as lending libraries, and even these were hardly known. Just as today, we helped ourselves to translations from English literature and I can still vividly remember my delight at finding an extensive series of books in the cupboard of my playmate's mother; a collection consisting of a number of such translated novels which had been compiled by a regional library.

In these books, I became acquainted with the experiences and suffering of countless Lords and Ladies, Sirs and Misses, details painstakingly described by writers of this nation, up to and including the colour of the garments worn by the hero or heroine at momentous occasions. Not merely the wedding outfits of the eternally blessed bride and groom but also those of the most distinguished guests would be immortalized. I was so enchanted with this literature that I could never get enough of it, since I was more limited by conventions than you are today. As soon as I had finished reading a voluminous work, I would feel rather lonely, as if a very dear and most interesting visitor had left.

All week I looked forward to Sunday afternoon because I would be able to indulge undisturbed in my favourite pastime. Impatient with passion, I feverishly followed the plot, but read more and more slowly when I noticed that I was coming to the end of the book, because I wanted to prolong the pleasure for as long as possible.

Richardson's novels[29] captivated me with delight, precisely because of their length. Although I never developed any particular fondness for the virtuous *Sir Charles Grandison* and I preferred the brilliant rascal Lovelace a thousand times more, I realize now that the works of this famous writer were not at all suited for a girl of barely twelve years of age, but so was the general consensus then. In fact, in England even the rather suggestive *Pamela* was praised from the pulpit as a devotional work. Besides, my father trusted in my innocence and rightly so. He was convinced that in my happy *naiveté* I would either overlook or misunderstand whatever was not appropriate for my age and his expectations did not deceive him.

Under these circumstances, my youthful, or rather my childish fantasies did not idle. My head was filled with seductions, masquerades, turbulent forced marriages; this technique used by English novelists of the time. It is similar to that used by their younger brothers today, who tend to repeat themselves and use the same formula. Now then, I tried to conform to these conventions in my own mind as well and so my hero was a formidable example of virtue, bravery, generosity and kindness. In other words, Grandison and Lovelace in one person.

As for myself I was a vivacious beauty, who lived in constant fear of pursuit from a variety of passionate admirers. Still, I remained a good child, studied my encyclopedias, knitted my stockings, sewed my clothes, helped my mother with the housework. No one could tell by looking at me, what strange thoughts permeated my mind.

This was just a delightful game to amuse me in my leisure hours. My hero did not have any form yet and could not have any form because I didn't know how to give him one. As I was not yet confirmed, I was not permitted to go out unaccompanied, so I did not know that many young men. However, the ones I did know did not appeal to me, likely because they did not pay attention to me.

The sentimental Siegwarts era that occurred soon after did not leave much of an impact on me. Although I did try to pick forget-me-nots and correspond with the pale moon. This worked quite well, only the matters about heartache troubled me somewhat. I did not know what to complain about to this distant sallow friend and I was too healthy and honest to invent a tale. And so I soon gave all this up and the submissive German heroine became proud English beauty once more.

Around the same time, *Sophie's Journey from Memel to Sachsen*[30] was published and this novel made an even greater impact on me. It goes without saying that I ignored the theological issues and controversies but for the first time in my life I was delighted to find old and dear friends in my books. The English lords and ladies never did become all that true to life for me, although I don't deny that they seemed all the more interesting for this very reason, because my imagination had more room to play. In contrast, I could visualize Puff and his associates sitting at my parents table and like Oelenschläger's *Correggio*[31], I felt a joyous wonder that someone could also paint such subjects.

Finally I was fourteen years old; about to make my entrance into womanhood when the dark hand of fate clouded my happy carefree life for the first time. Just when I needed her gentle direction the most, I lost my dear, loving, and wonderful mother.

She passed away as softly and gently as she had lived, robbed from us by a gradual illness that since the birth of my sister had been slowly and almost imperceptibly consuming her until she finally collapsed without complaint. All that time she had caressed us with sweet hopes for an almost perfect recovery.

Still half-child, I was beside myself with shock and pain as I stood beside her casket, in that same room where just a few days before we had been so happy together. The walls were draped in black now and I hardly recognized the room. I held my little sister in my arms while she, in her childish innocence, smiled at the numerous candles that brightened the room. For the last time, they would illuminate that dear, soundless pale form.

Next to me stood my despairing father. For the first time in my life, I saw a man with tears in his eyes. It was incomprehensibly painful to see him cry openly; an unnatural phenomenon, it seemed to me and the blood froze in my veins. In any case, funeral arrangements at that time only served to heighten an overwhelming pain and making outward appearances intolerable.

Not just Father and the children, but all our servants were wrapped in black crepe. And for the first week I was not permitted to remove the long trailing veil or the wide black headdress that almost concealed my face; not even at home.

Until after the day of the burial, all windows of our house were tightly closed, and sitting room, stairway and entrance were draped in black. People dressed in black crept silently as ghosts in the gloomy twilight. The pain we felt required this; the customs of the day demanded this.

And when I looked at the lovely pale face of my mother in the midst of this gloomy splendour! How this image of death assaulted my young soul; I felt as if I would die of pain and horror. I thought I would never be able to be happy again and yet the power of time triumphs over everything. This is especially true for the young and I must confess that I became calm and cheerful again much sooner than I expected.

Even father soon regained his composure and was able to bear his loss although he was never able to recover from the loss of his wife because he loved her very much. Forthright and sensitive, she was, as most well-situated women of her time, merely the echo to her husband's freer, stronger character. Her husband was a deity. *My husband said* or *the master has ordered that* . . . in her mind, these were fundamental statements that no reasonable person would dispute. Though she was far from being slavish or submissive; it was simply impossible for this dear heart to imagine anyone finer than her husband.

From now on, my share of Father's love and care doubled and sometimes tripled. He could only gaze at my little sister with a quiet sadness and she remained at home in the care of our nursemaid, who had also taken care of me when I was a child. For twenty-four years she had faithfully served our family and had earned the right to be considered a family member and was occasionally permitted take part in important discussions.

The death of my mother had postponed my confirmation by several months, and in my current bereft and forlorn condition, this important milestone was more important to me than ever, and it was truly a most significant milestone. For from that day forward, not only would I be considered an independent member of society, but at the same time I would also take over command of our rather considerable household. To the best of my ability, I would be expected to replace the position of my late mother.

After surviving the first wave of pain over the death of my mother, the feeling that she was irreplaceable was never so heart wrenching as on the moment when we returned from the funeral ceremony to an empty house. How I yearned for an embrace, an open heart that would understand, but there was no one to comfort me.

I found myself in a very singular emotional state. Never before had I felt this way. Certainly, I had been impressed by the religious aspect of the ceremony that I had just attended, but it had left me emotionally distant. The brief, though intense feelings that had seized me today soon gave way to a certain vanity. A little smugly, I recalled having survived this test and having demonstrated my superiority to all the others. Considering all the Bible verses I had to learn by heart to prove my beliefs, my memory did not fail to serve me. However, not one verse had commanded my heart, for since childhood, true piety, even the concept of piety, was unknown to me. I had depended on my memory to learn about religion, the same way I had studied geography and history. So the spirit of religion had never penetrated me to any significant depth. Until then, I had never heard anyone speak of God, other than at church, which we had attended sometimes.

Dear children, do not wonder about my confession. Instead, criticize the cold bleak time that was my childhood, a time when people began to be ashamed of religion. Since the beginning of time, one fabrication has always blazed the trail for opposing fabrications. And so, the gaudy flicker of comfortless scepticism suddenly penetrated this gloomy darkness where just before the most garish superstition had ruled. It was called *Enlightenment* then. It was only natural that those multitudes blinded by this abrupt transition from darkness to cold northern glare should abandon their path for another erroneous path. Indeed, how could they envision that there was a correct path?

The most intelligent people of that time, my father included, let themselves be carried away by Voltaire's cold but sparkling wit; a wit that ruthlessly mocked both the sacred and profane.

A dreadful numbing coldness began to control belief and understanding and Voltaire's followers boasted loudly that they would acknowledge only the religion of an honest man; *la religion d'un homme honnête*, as they called it. Unfortunately my father belonged to this group.

My extremely pious mother, who had been brought up in quiet simplicity, was silent about all of this out of devotion to my father. She never contradicted his view; this was easier for her because no one intruded upon the quiet course she had chosen. This was the basic principle of those enlightened ones; to leave women and other people with their misconceptions and delusions, as they called these viewpoints, for as long as they wished to remain with them.

As for myself, my mother consoled herself that I received proper daily religious instruction from a student of theology. My mother, for her part, enjoyed the freedom of quietly distancing herself whenever the bubbling French wit of my father's company went too much against the grain of what was sacred to her.

Without direction from my dear mother, without emotional support of any kind, I became rather solitary and impoverished. I knew nothing about transcendence over earthly pain through the guidance from an incomprehensible, merciful and mighty force and yet in my heart I believed in its power. I was not irreligious, I did not reject religion, I was simply *nothing*. No call had summoned and brought to life the dormant goodness in my heart.

Now that I am a woman of almost sixty years, I hope you will not think I am vain when I tell you frankly that a long, long time ago, I was very attractive. When I look at you, Victorine, you remind me of my younger self. But don't be cross when I say that my long soft blond tresses were silkier and more abundant than your brown hair, my radiant blue eyes more expressive than your brown eyes, my complexion more fair, and my figure more elegant and shapely. Enough! In spite of the crippling fashion of the time, I distinguished myself very conspicuously from my friends. Look at me carefully, children. See how quickly splendour and glory pass away in this world.

My dear father now looked at his child not just with vanity but with a certain pride as well, drawing attention to these little advantages in a way that is only excusable because of a father's love. He had truly loved my unassuming gentle mother. At her side, he had been indescribably happy. And yet he was led astray by this vanity to raise me contrary to what my mother was.

He was reminded of his youth, most of which he spent in Paris in the *salons* of those intelligent ladies, whose opinions dominated half of Europe in those days. Madame du Deffand, the learned Lespinasse, Madame de Tencin, and many others, who with their spirit, wit, talent and charm created an intellectual centre in the middle of this frivolous turmoil of a floundering nation. But who remembers their names today?

Just when the exuberance of youth surrenders easily and willingly to every flattering influence, my father sunned himself in the rays of their intellect. Somewhere in the depths of his soul, he had preserved a good many wonderful memories, which a father's love now somehow confused with his daughter's own character. And so he deluded himself into following a plan whereby he would do everything possible to transform me into something akin to those famous ladies, even if my radius of my brilliance would only extend to far more limited sphere.

At any rate, by way of readings and verbal instruction, he wanted to enlighten me regarding every exalted prejudice and from that day on, he made this his life's work. My natural abilities, combined with my vanity, which was freshly animated by my father (which should perhaps be pardonable in my present circumstances) supported his endeavours. In fact, in just a few years I bloomed into quite a dazzling beauty and still, aroused by all the stimulating qualities of the outside world, my perceptive mind and quick wit made no less of an impression.

The girls and young ladies with whom I had associated until now did not join me as often, perhaps they even avoided me because they found my company depressing. And yet I did not mind this all that much because the familiarity of this intimate circle had become increasingly monotonous to me.

In any case, almost imperceptibly our way of life had changed completely after the death of my mother. Our acquaintance with so many of the most prominent families of the city, as I described earlier, gradually ended all by itself, somewhat like the swinging of a pendulum in a faltering clock that never stops abruptly.

If frequently remaining at home means devotion to home life, then our lives were far more domestic than in the days when my mother was still living with us. We hardly ever went out. Instead, every day a small but carefully selected group of witty gentlemen gathered in our house.

An unexpected and somewhat considerable inheritance made it possible for us to entertain with controlled elegance, sparing us from showy extravagance and fearful thriftiness. Every day we welcomed artists, scholars, and interesting gentlemen from every profession. Even today, the city hides many more of these kinds of gentlemen than one would believe.

Many strangers joined our circle; in fact, no man of any importance would spend longer than a day in the city without seeking admission to it. Foreign artists from all nations sought us, many of whom hoped to attain a higher degree of recognition through association with us. Gladly and willingly, they provided their talents, adding a new zest to our informal evenings.

Meanwhile, I had grown accustomed to and felt quite at ease with these visitors to my father's home, who were most pleased when I acknowledged them. In turn, our guests raced each other to praise me and many claimed quite frankly that I would attract attention and admiration in every court, even in Paris.

My head was spinning with all this flattery but I was most delighted for my father's sake, for I now loved him more than ever. His quiet pleasure over my exceptional success in society did not escape my sharp eyes and I saw very clearly the secret look of triumph glistening in his eyes as he followed my every movement.

Often, when I raised my voice fearlessly to express an opinion with well-chosen phrases about some current literary subject under discussion, father would always be the first to try to direct the attention of our guests my way. He listened more closely than anyone else did, when I condemned some theory or other relating to the dominant moral philosophy or political thoughts of the time. Already then, sermons of freedom and equality could be heard.

He rewarded me with a smile of approval whenever I mercilessly pursued inconsistencies with my facile wit or when I involved myself in intense exchanges where I was invariably the winner. In those situations, my unusual mental agility may have given me a sort of superiority, but often the victory was due to the courtesy of my opponents which was customary at the time. Old-fashioned, they were much too gallant to dispute in earnest with a lady.

So in the bloom of innocent youth, I was surrounded by a flock of men, all of whom flattered me with their attention, each according to his own method. I sat among them like a little queen without rivals for my sister was still too young to appear at our dinner parties and little by little my female friends had distanced themselves from me. I neither missed them nor was I alienated by their absence, for I knew from my father that in their time, the prominent ladies in Paris were just as alone, surrounded by their male circle as I was now.

Certainly, my father's position among the diplomats in our city obliged me to sometimes appear at rare larger festive occasions where both sexes were invited, but here too, I maintained my position. I was too conspicuous and recognized as *nonpareil*[32] in every respect, so it would never have occurred to anyone to challenge me.

As soon as I left the house, my admirers formed a corral around me and those who were not able to penetrate the circle, basked in my rays from a distance.

In all my innocence, I was actually rather coquettish, if being so means wanting to please everyone without any sense of discretion. In truth, this is what I wanted, but only because I had not met a man, whom I would select above all his peers for a place in my heart.

All the men I knew were the same to me, but I regarded them as my subjects and they were not permitted to rebel or show signs of disloyalty. My true purpose was to please my father, not only because he was my father, but because he was the finest and most brilliant man I knew. I was proud to listen to him and to be the pride and joy of this venerable man was my greatest happiness.

The image of his own youthful years, as I imagined them became my ideal and I refused many marriage proposals simply because the men pursuing me were too different from my father. I did not value any of them enough as a future son-in-law for my father. These young men who crowded around me, all seemed a little dull to me. I couldn't help thinking that another vanity greater than my own was gathering at the steps to my throne. Essentially, I did not attach much value to their tributes and that is why I paid too little attention to them. Still, it amused me when I was able to entertain myself with their foolishness. I treated them like marionettes, bestowing life and mobility at my whim.

Time passed and days became weeks and weeks became months and months became years and I was never particularly aware it. I was almost twenty-three years old when, in the middle of the most beautiful time of the year, the air was filled with a half-fearful half-joyful tension. The innocent cause of this excitement was the reigning Duchess von P. who was on her way to a resort and intended to visit us briefly with her two daughters. She had decided to spend a few days in our city in order to view the points of interest and especially to acquaint herself with the beautiful surrounding area.

Forty years ago, travelling was more difficult than it is today where it has become more and more like a pleasant outing. There were few reputable inns, and few tolerable, let alone paved roads. So most people, if they were not required to travel, were glad to remain at home. In those days, it was rare for kings and princes to travel. For this reason, long in advance of the arrival of the crowned head, all windows that looked out towards the street would be appropriated.

The inquisitive masses crowded head to head in tight rows around the imposing majestic carriage and old people who in their youth had the pleasure of viewing an emperor or king from a distance, would tell their children and grandchildren about this event, as if this was actually the most spellbinding moment of their lives.

The mere passing through of the duchess would have been enough to set the city in motion, but now that she wanted to spend three entire days among us, lively festivities would take place. This was no small task for those who had to come up with the arrangements. Certainly, even in this city the fondness for luxury had escalated in the last ten years. Little by little, significant changes had been made to the citizens' traditional way of life but the idea of courtyard festivities was still too unfamiliar to be automatically adopted by the freethinking citizens of this imperial city.

While the men consulted with my father and proposed how to receive and entertain the Princess, the women were no less employed preparing their own finery for this grand occasion.

Probably I was the idlest woman in the entire city at this time because the obsession to shine in this way was never one of my aspirations. Instead, proudly cognisant of my assets, I dressed with subtle elegance to eclipse the radiance of my rivals glittering with precious stones, silver and tinsel. This time too, I promised to remain true to my accustomed habit.

In spite of this, my heart beat faster when I thought that I would be presented to a princess. Although I had never seen a princess, a king or even an emperor would not have created such a stir within me, because emperors and kings are men and I knew how to relate to men. I could even hope to be just as attractive to them as I would be to other men. However, a duchess, a princess! Well, that was quite another matter. The mere thought of someone who was so similar to and simultaneously so different from me, filled me with apprehension and awe. In vain, I taxed my brain trying to fathom how a princess who had grown up in an entirely different sphere and with very different perceptions could appear among us, where she actually did not belong and would have to comply, just as any other young lady would.

Finally, the big day arrived and the Princess appeared and among others I was presented to her in the row of first ladies of the city. Although this was a rather uncomplicated ceremony, for the first time in my life I was extremely self-conscious and was secretly very annoyed with myself about this. Somehow, I was unable to shake off this sudden fearful timidity. The Princess was a beautiful tall motherly-looking woman and appeared to be the epitome of kindness and graciousness. In fact, she was dressed far less elaborately than we were and wore neither jewelry or other ornament.

With a skilled ease that she learned at a young age, the Princess turned to each lady in turn and had a pleasant word for each one. I was especially honoured by her attention to me when she asked about several of my relatives, whom she had known in earlier times and I replied as well as I was able to, but my voice was shaky, my cheeks glowed, and my eyes were glued to the ground.

She averted any possibility of aristocratic condescension and her noble poise impressed me very much; this remarkable dignity that appeared to animate her personality. Her cornflower blue eyes, though mildly beaming, seemed to pierce into the depths of my soul. I was probably not the first awkward figure, such as I appeared, to stand before her, because I had the impression that she understood my situation. With compassion, she attempted to relieve my uneasiness by directing me to her daughters, two delicate ethereal creatures. The youngest, Princess Mathilde, a child of twelve years, looked dream-like as a sylph.

I felt the intent of the Princess and was even more ashamed of my foolish conduct, however by and by I regained reasonable composure while talking with the young ladies, although I was a long way off from my usual confident self.

At last, I dared to look up again, but then I shrank back in alarm because the first thing I saw was a young man standing very close behind the Princess. Meeting my eyes, he glanced quickly away, blushing almost imperceptibly and I also cast my eyes down again and felt my cheeks turn dark crimson. When I was certain that I was no longer being observed, I looked furtively in his direction again and glimpsed at a tall and aristocratic figure. He was very handsome with an expressive serious look on his face. His quiet unassuming yet genteel demeanour showed that he was cultured; a man of the world.

Looking from him to my numerous admirers who were beginning to fill the room, I was never less pleased with them than I was today. They all stood at a respectful distance and some, likely feeling even more awkward than I was feeling, huddled against the wall. At this moment, I wished for nothing more than to discover the identity of this interesting stranger. But where would I find the courage to ask about him? All of a sudden, I had become a silly awkward child and I hardly recognized myself.

It had been planned that the Princess would be given a tour of some of the most beautiful points of interest in the surrounding area. She graciously invited me to accompany her daughter. The Princess, her housemaid and I sat together in an open carriage, while the stranger drove beside the Princess's wagon. He seemed to be bound to her in some way, as if he were not permitted to depart from her side.

Meanwhile, I had the opportunity to observe him from a distance. Mounted on his horse, his elegant form was seen to best advantage. As the old saying goes, the horse is for men, the equivalent of the ballroom for ladies; a place where physical attributes may be displayed to the best advantage.

With quiet delight, I was aware that he looked around for us, whenever the opportunity presented itself. I noticed this each time it happened, but still did not have the courage to ask for his name.

At the end of the sight-seeing excursion, a simple but elegant meal had been planned in one of the most beautiful gardens in the outskirts of the city. Later in the evening, the grand finale to the day's happy festivities would be a brilliant display of fireworks, presented by a master of this art.

For this purpose, a platform covered with a silk canopy had been specially built for the Princess. A few steps down from this platform led to the garden below and a few steps down from the house, on the main level was the large triple window glass entrance to the dining hall. Here, seating had been arranged for the Princess and the ladies. At the end of the second row of chairs, I found my own place, not far from where the Princess was seated.

The fireworks commenced and the warm summer night was perfect for this kind of entertainment. Dark clouds covered the horizon, but there was no threat of rain. The fiery multi-hued riotous blasts of constantly changing colours was a passionate magical splendour; a striking contrast to this sombre background.

The expressions on the faces of the numerous onlookers, some in the garden, grouped around the canopy, some standing, some sitting, all dressed in their finest clothes, only heightened the fascination of this magical spectacle. Sometimes the crowded heads would be illuminated by the brightest of lights, sometimes they would fade away, disappearing into the dark mysteries of the night.

To the delight of everyone present, the fireworks were a grand sensation. The last sparkling burst was about to appear; the brightest fiery pillar of brilliance. A flaming eagle was to fly over the platform, up to one of the windows, in order to ignite the noble monogrammed letters there. Everyone waited in suspended anticipation. But the eagle would not reach the middle of the course because one of the wires which held it in place snapped. The blazing mass suddenly bounced plummeting backward right to where the Princess was seated, setting the silk canopy on fire and injuring a few ladies before landing in the middle of the floor of the platform, spreading a steaming, hissing, crackling fear and danger among the spectators.

It is difficult to describe how everything came to an end amid the tumult, clamour, and chaos. Such mayhem is unimaginable; it must be experienced. For the moment, courtesy and consideration were forgotten. People thought only of themselves and those closest to themselves. Those on the platform, charged into one another in mad confusion blocking access to the dining hall. The piercing cry of calls for loved ones was deafening, but the fear of losing someone in this crushing horde was very real.

The atmosphere of sheer panic only increased the general frenzy. Of course the danger emanating from this panic could have been anticipated and prevented by a single level- headed man, who could have easily seized the smouldering drapery and kicked the burning eagle away into the garden. But this was not the case and now it was too late.

The flimsy battens which had formed a kind of balustrade around the platform were now completely demolished by people responding to the cries of wives and daughters, and in desperation grasped the battens to ascend from the garden. In this tumult, chairs were overturned, and some people fell over these in their flight, while others tripped on the steps leading up to the house, tripping those following them.

Fortunately, the Princess had fled to the house right at the beginning of the turmoil. Three seconds later, stampedes of people blocked all three entrances to the house. In minutes, in fact in less time than it took me to tell you about this calamity, everything came to a standstill, no one could move forwards or backwards and everywhere there were the terrible deafening screams of people in hysteria.

Luckily, I was able to remain calm and recognizing the futility of panic compounded with fear of escalating danger, I did not run towards the house as the others did. A swift jump sideways off the low platform and I would be able to escape into the soft grass of the almost vacant garden. I knew I could find my way around in the darkness because I was quite familiar with the area since childhood. There, I planned to wait quietly until the worst of the situation had subsided.

But just as I was gathering my dress and preparing myself to jump, I felt a gentle force pressing against my knees. Startled, I looked down and was hardly able to trust my eyes. There, completely helpless and trembling uncontrollably as she clasped my knees, was little Princess Mathilde lying on the floor of the platform, among the overturned chairs. Separated from her mother right at the beginning of the confusion, the poor girl had tripped over the chairs and no one had noticed.

Although several people were responsible for her care, in the commotion no one looked after her, because each party assumed that someone else had ensured for her safety, thereby leaving her completely exposed to being either trampled or smothered by the crowd.

I immediately accepted responsibility for the delicate little girl, kneeling down at the edge of the platform, I carefully lowered her to the grass below. Then I jumped down myself.

The tumultuous noise above seemed to be worse and the child lay at my feet as if unconscious. I was about to try to revive her with some *Eau de Luce* from the flask I had with me, when suddenly I was shaken by successive violent explosions.

In a flash, a rain of fire illuminated the night. Hundreds of fiery serpents flew hissing and crackling through the air in all directions, spreading a hair-raising eerie brightness that alternated with a dense black.

By accident, a huge number of separate rockets had ignited. The intention had been to combine them into a gigantic candelabrum for the grand *finale* of the fireworks celebration. Probably the fireworks artist panicked in all the turmoil. This unhappy culmination to the first misfortune was certainly not his fault, rather likely occurred by servants with torches who were desperately searching for their masters and mistresses.

By now I was so unnerved by the screaming, the explosions, the incessant shower of sparks overhead, and the fiery rockets spinning around us, that I felt very vulnerable in an increasingly dangerous situation. Though I was terribly frightened, I tried to maintain a sense of composure and took the almost unconscious child in my arms. She felt as light as a feather.

I remembered there was a garden house far away from the turmoil and I thought I could bring the two of us there. The garden house would offer relative safety for the time being.

Already, cold raindrops were falling and the night sky was shrouded darker than before. Shivering with trepidation, I carried my burden as swiftly as I could towards this garden house. I had already covered some distance carrying the child when in my haste and fear I missed a few steps that led to a low level terrace. I slipped and fell down these steps with the child in my arms. To my horror, I realized immediately that I could not get up to go further.

The garden was dark and deathly quiet. The fireworks seemed to have worn itself out by now. Only a dull undulating din came from the distant platform. The rain began to splash noisily around us, waking the little princess. She shivered like an aspen leaf, but was happy to find me holding her.

"Miss," she pleaded in tears. "Dear Miss, please get up, so that we can go to my mother." When she realized that I was not able to get up, she cried out in heart-rending distress for help as loudly as she could. In vain, I tried to comfort her, but she would not let me and shivered violently. I assured her that all danger had passed, and that the pain in my foot would soon go away, so that I would soon be able to bring her home safely, since I knew the way.

It was all for nothing. Her anxiety only increased and she cried more loudly than before. The poor girl was in such distress that I could hear her teeth chattering and I felt pity for the little thing.

We did not wear shawls in those days so I tore off my *circassienne,* a type of robe that was in fashion then. I wrapped the heavy silk fabric around the poor princess, in effort to protect her from the rain that was beginning to pour down with increasing force. In gratitude, she wrapped her delicate little arms around my neck, and buried her face in my shoulder, crying and sobbing softly all the while.

Then suddenly she began to scream hysterically for help with twice the intensity as before. Princess Mathilde's unnatural ferocity alarmed me. I was truly afraid for the both of us now.

The pain in my foot was getting worse by the minute and the rain was falling harder all the time. Without even my *circassienne* to cover me, I was in danger of getting thoroughly drenched.

You can imagine my relief when I saw the reflection of light coming from the yew hedge that enclosed the terrace. The princess also recognized this light as a ray of hope and stood up, turning towards the direction of its apparent origin.

Instantly she cheered with renewed energy,

"Leuen, dear Leuen, here! Mathilde is down here! Miss Falkenhayn is also here! Hurry, help us! Here!"

The bushes above me rustled and a man jumped down from the upper terrace. He was holding a lantern that he likely appropriated from a house somewhere so I was able to see straight away that he was the man who had accompanied the Duchess.

"Thank God that I have found you, Princess!" he exclaimed, completely out of breath. "We all thought that we would find you at home. The Princess is beside herself with worry over you. Come, we must hurry. Allow me to carry you to the carriage, so that can get along more quickly."

"No, no, no, no!" cried the little princess anxiously. "Look here. Our poor dear Miss Falkenhayn has broken her foot, because she had to carry me. Oh God! She is going to die! Look how pale she has become all of a sudden. She will surely die, if she doesn't get help right away." The poor girl started to cry again and embraced me as I was still lying on the ground.

The stranger who noticed me for the first time, was visibly upset, and seemed to be searching for words after the initial shock.

"It is not as serious, as Princess Mathilde believes," I interjected and tried to force a smile in spite of the tremendous pain in my foot. "I slipped and sprained my foot, perhaps twisted it a little, but it's not broken, I hope. I think I can manage the few steps to the carriage." I tried to get up. Herr von Leuen supported me and with compassion little Mathilde summoned the bit of strength she had to help me. But I was overcome with pain, and barely able to contain my cry, I sank back into the grass.

"It's no use," I said, trying to conceal my pain as well as I could. "It's no use, Herr von Leuen. Kindly bring the Princess to the carriage and then send help for me."

"No, no, no!" cried the Princess once again as she entwined her arms around me, clutching me very tightly as if someone wanted to remove her by force. "No, Leuen, don't do this. Whatever happens, I cannot leave my dear kind protectress all alone."

"I also cannot agree with that decision," answered von Leuen not without some emotion. "But what should we do? The weather is taking a turn for the worse. What should we do?"

At that moment, he saw people at some distance wandering about with torches. Presumably, they were still looking for the Princess. Von Leuen shouted as loudly as he was able but the howling of the wind and the hard impact of the rain was too great. No one heard him.

The lights had moved further away and then disappeared completely. The Princess would not permit Herr von Leuen to look for them and she held him back with tears. No one came to look for us. Who would imagine that we would be in this very secluded area of the garden?

"If the Princess would be willing, there are barely a hundred steps to where I would be able to call for the carriage," von Leuen began a little awkwardly.

"Oh, yes, I can! I can!" cried the child in a trembling voice. "Nothing is wrong with me, dear Leuen. Just help Miss Falkenhayn and give me the lantern to carry. You can carry her in your arms, just as she carried me before."

"The Princess is right. Please trust me, Miss Falkenhayn," said Von Leuen. Although his noticeably trembling voice betrayed inner confusion, he did not wait for my reply, but simply lifted me up with his strong arms. His actions almost took my breath away, but what could I do? I lay in his arms, pressed to his chest like a child. His breath blew against my cheek and I heard every beat of his heart.

At that moment, a nameless confidence I had never experienced before filled my soul and I found myself trusting this stranger, whose name I hardly knew. I didn't know why, but my eyes filled with warm soothing tears. He noticed my quiet weeping.

"You are suffering so much," he whispered with an indescribably soothing gentle voice and I could see by the light of the lantern carried by the Princess that a moist shimmer intensified the beauty of his eyes. I was not able to answer his question.

Our progress was very slow. Poor little Mathilde could not walk very well and Herr von Leuen had to take his time with the extra weight he was obliged to carry.

Finally, we reached the carriage and our protector sat down beside me so that he could support me a little. In an effort to minimize the impact, he directed the driver to drive slowly.

Mathilde sat on the opposite side and insisted that I put my sore foot on her lap, chattering all the while with the happiness of a child who believes that she has experienced something most extraordinary and is very relieved to have escaped a great danger. It seems that she was more aware of her surroundings than I had believed at the time, because she was now able to relate every detail of how I had lowered her from the platform, jumped down afterwards and then carried her and finally how I had torn my *circassienne* to protect her from the cold and rain.

When she related this last detail, I suddenly realized the tattered condition of my dress, now fully visible by the light of the lanterns on the carriage and I could feel the blood rise to my face. Von Leuen, who had been watching me closely the whole time, noticed me blushing and I saw that he too began to turn red. He quickly looked away and avoided looking at me again until the carriage stopped at the home of the Princess.

As light as a bird, and with a cheerful shout, Princess Mathilde flew down from the carriage, ran up the steps of the house and into the arms of her mother. I requested that I be brought to my father, but just then, he approached the carriage and embraced me with loving concern.

He had not gone to the fireworks display because the evening air was not good for his health but when he heard about the somewhat exaggerated rumours of the fireworks disaster, and I failed to return, his worry drove him to the Princess, where he had hoped to find me. Both now shared their concern over the fate of their children and hope for their rescue. Everyone available was sent to look for us but no one thought to look in the garden. Only Herr von Leuen, who incidentally was not at all familiar with the garden, was brought to our aid by a happy coincidence. Oddly, no one understood how Princess Mathilde found herself in this predicament. But it was quite obvious upon reflection. When someone's care is entrusted to many, often this person is the first to be neglected. This is most obvious during important events, when each servant depends too much upon the careful vigilance of the other servants.

While the Princess was occupied with the happiness of finding her lost child, I was carried into one of her rooms. In my condition, she would not allow me to be brought to the rather distant apartment of my father.

The Princess soon came to see me herself. With warm tears of gratitude, she embraced me and thanked me for saving her daughter. As many grown-ups who seldom involve themselves with life's smaller mishaps, she exaggerated the danger as well, floating with the Princess in awe of what I had done. Of course, these same people often endure more serious misfortune with a courage that would put many of us to shame.

The Princess said that I was an angel sent from Heaven to protect her daughter and tirelessly praised my courage, prudence and self-sacrifice that at last I was almost ashamed of myself. What was it exactly that enabled someone to reach the clouds? What was so great about what I had done? I was sober-minded enough to take care of myself with relatively good common sense and not so inhumane that I could have abandoned a dear, weak, and helpless child.

When the Princess left, all those remaining in the room, from her personal maid to the lower ranking servants, simultaneously exaggerated these accolades to an ever higher degree, telling each other about the wonders I had worked. I began to get rather bored with it all and tried to portray my own impression of what had occurred, but I was preaching to deaf ears and was praised all the more loudly for my modesty. Finally, I said nothing at all, and patiently endured their attentions and soon discovered that this was the best way to silence these somewhat boisterous parrots.

Meanwhile, the Princess's doctor examined my injured foot. As I had guessed earlier, it was not broken, only twisted and very swollen. The doctor promised a complete recovery in a matter of a few days, on the condition that I did not exert any pressure on my foot.

So going back home with my father would not be possible and the Princess insisted upon accepting complete charge of my care. Unfortunately, our nocturnal adventure had given Princess Mathilde a cold and slight fever, and her mother's health had suffered as well with emotional turmoil of the evening. In any case, the Princess was now obliged to extend her stay in this region indefinitely. Perhaps she was simply exhausted or needed an excuse to escape from other festivities that had been planned for her.

My own recovery took longer than the doctor had hoped for when he first saw me, so I ended up staying with the Princess for two complete weeks. This sojourn became a highlight of my life and the reflection of it still illuminates the darkness of my old age.

Then, I thought a stroke of magic had transported me to a completely new world. All my concepts about myself and life in general took a totally new direction. At least for the moment, all that had amused me and all that had blinded me before had now disappeared from my eyes.

Despite the benevolent indulgence of the Princess, I felt so subordinate to her in every respect that it never would have occurred to me to continue playing my usual brilliant role in her presence. And the quiet, serious, almost timid modesty of the older Princess Ludovika, who was only a few years younger than I was, created a sense of reticence in me that I had not known before.

It is not that I was pretending or trying to appear to be other than I was. No! I remained open and sincere as always because it was my character to be so, not because I was virtuous. I simply did as I always did, taking my cue from my surroundings at a particular moment. With little Princess Mathilde, who clung to me passionately, I played the high-spirited child and in the presence of Princess Ludovika and their mother, I adapted myself to the modest attitude and unassuming demeanour displayed by them. Not one of my admirers would have recognized me after this transformation, I had changed so completely from the way I was before the fireworks and I am convinced I was never more charming than I was during my stay in that house. I was quite aware of this and was quite happy about it, but unfortunately I was not wise enough then to draw a lesson from this time that would apply to my future life.

The remainder of the Princess's travel plans was reduced to the minimum possible for someone of her position. Furthermore, essential household staff was comprised of a lady-in-waiting who had lived together with the Princess since her youth, her personal housemaid, her escort and the doctor.

Baron Reineck, a middle-aged man, only arrived after the fireworks. An unexpected coincidence created a chance meeting with his beloved sister, whom he had not seen for many years and the Princess permitted him to stay with his sister for a few days. This was why Herr von Leuen, who also happened to be there, offered to serve as replacement for his friend Baron Reineck during his absence. In any case, for business reasons he had thought to spend a few days in our city. He had spent part of last winter at the Princess's residence and she had found him to be a very pleasant companion, so she was completely satisfied with the prospect of having him serve as escort. Even now, after the return of Baron Reineck, she would not hear of him taking another apartment and as part of her invitation, he was to remain with us.

I can say "us" because in those happy days, I too could count myself as a member of the Princess's little circle. All of us who belonged to this little group would gather every evening in the Princess's salon, which remained closed to all other visitors under the pretext of Princess Mathilde's illness. What fun we had those evenings!

How impatiently I would wait until the hour when the Princess returned after having fulfilled her obligations to attend dinner with the important people of the city. What a thrill it was to see her two towering servants enter my room in theatrically colourful attire, ready to carry me from my day bed to their mistress.

Subtle conventions prevailed in this little evening circle and yet all compulsions, all etiquette considered absolutely essential by the world's elite were banned here. It was the most appropriate answer to Tasso's not yet written maxim: "If you want to learn precisely what is proper, ask only noble women."

Each one of us participated according to individual sense of humour, purpose, skill, talent and the Princess hovered over all of us, stimulating us with her calm genius. Never had I seen a woman who was always able to direct a conversation with such unassuming grace so that the experience was enjoyable for everyone present. Nor have I seen a woman since, who understood the art of listening so well.

She absolutely detested all forms of social banter that ended in bitter personal assaults. Still, the most avant-garde wit had free rein as long as the intention was to amuse and not to wound. In her presence, no one was permitted to feel brushed-off, dejected, mistreated or affronted.

I marvelled at the Princess. She was so very different from those women in Paris. Those women whom my father had often described and extolled as the epitome of female perfection! For the first time in my life I had an indication that youth, beauty, intelligence, wit, and the gift of being able to speak in an interesting manner about every subject was by far not everything that one needs in order to love and be loved. Indeed, I sensed that a more reliable and enduring fulfilment to these dreams was possible with far fewer dazzling charms when we approach people with genuine kindness, and unaffected benevolence.

In our little social circle, Bernhard von Leuen occupied a position of distinction next to the Princess. It was obvious that despite his youth, he followed his own steady path with self-assurance. He was not immediately lead astray by one foolish notion after another.

Although he had the benefits of an exemplary education and possessed other important advantages, he did not display any signs of ambition or desire for attention or admiration. Essentially, his nature appeared to be led by a certain deliberate tranquillity, which prevented him from jostling for position anywhere. He rather took things in stride and was not one to stand in awe.

Polite to everyone, especially to ladies, he nevertheless differentiated himself from the somewhat monotonous manner of both younger and older gentlemen of the time, by showing us the honour or justice of treating us as intelligent individuals and not as children. Although he was not actually humorous, he embellished every meaningful conversation with his most unique and wonderful gift of words.

Whenever any particularly honourable emotion inspired him, the magic of his persuasion enraptured even the coldest of hearts. Everyone felt that what was most compelling was not his careful choice of words, or the unusually rich and pure tone of his voice; there was a depth of meaning that was not conveyed in words alone.

What he said was not merely the product of a bright mind, it sprung from the bottom of an understanding heart and therefore what he said went straight to the hearts of others. He had done a lot of travelling and had seen the finest and most noble sights that the world has to offer. A kind learned man had taught him how to adapt his observations to both expand his knowledge as well as to prepare him for practical living and we were able to see that he was fully aware of what the world demanded from him, and what he in turn demanded of the world.

Do not chastise an old heart for warming itself in this somewhat verbose outpouring of praises for my old friend. He was exactly as I have described him to you. I never saw anyone like him, and will never see anyone like him again. The Princess desired that he read to us and he did this at least for one hour daily and we all treasured every word he uttered; watching every refined expression.

Through him, I first became acquainted with German poetry, and the rich eloquence that our language is capable of, though I had been completely unaware of this until then. Remember that until then, with the exception of a few English and Italian classics, my father had acquainted me mainly with French literature. Most of our German writers were foreign to me, especially the unique poetry of this country that was slowly emerging after a long absence.

It seemed to me that the Princess and Bernhard von Leuen savoured my joyful surprise with the same benevolent and hospitable sensation that we experience the first time we show a friend the nicest spot in a delightful place already well-known to us or when we set before him a beautiful work of art that he has never seen before. We relive the pleasure he feels at that particular moment and remember when we stood for first time where he is standing now.

But this is all in the past! And now, feeling rather melancholic about the transience of man, of worldly greatness and fame, I am forced to witness how the accomplishments of these men, of whom we should be eternally proud, are already wasted by their ungrateful grandchildren.

How long until all is completely forgotten; disappeared? And then, perhaps in a spirit of fashionable misinterpretation, we will ferret out the songs of journeymen and collect and admire them as masterpieces. How many young book-devouring readers today know of Kleist's *Frühling*[33]other than through hearsay? But every half-educated Englishman knows his Thomson almost by heart and new editions appear every year in his memory. Even Klopstock[34], who lived among us until a few years ago is gradually slipping into oblivion. We refer to him out of habit or with a kind of reverence, but how many people today know more than just his name? It's the same with Hagedorn, Utz, Cronegk, Haller, Hölty, and so many others. We ought to be ashamed that foreigners will soon know them better than we do, while our voracious appetite gorges itself on the latest products, daily newspapers and paperbacks that upon conception already carry the germ of transience. They are not even required to live longer than the moment of origin; the moment for which they were created.

With an indefinable sense of awareness, I listened to individual songs read from his then recent *Messiah* and the comments from Von Leuen and the Princess seized me with no less sense of wonder. Referring to sacred entities was entirely new to me and I did not understand much of what was being discussed or read. And yet I was somehow inexplicably moved by an emotion I had never felt before.

Sometimes I felt inspired, as though I was transcending myself and for the first time in my life a warm radiance took hold of me, which has now become a comfort in my age; its soft light illuminates the dark path that I will soon have to cross.

As fascinated and inspired as I was by what was going on, I must confess however, that my feminine nature would not let me refrain from noticing the pleasure in Bernhard's eyes whenever he glanced my way thinking himself to be undetected.

It became apparent to me that his expression and intonation demonstrated that the most beautiful, tender and poignant verses of poems that he loved and knew by heart were meant for me alone. Even if doubts still crossed my mind, the secretive smiles of the people present and certain casual remarks only reinforced my observations.

Certainly he was not an *homme aux petits soins*, and I could not imagine anything more touching than these thousand little almost imperceptible courtesies that were invariably directed towards me. Often I saw his face turn pale when occasionally the pain in my foot suddenly recurred and I would twinge with a cry could not suppress.

That prophesying voice, that lives in the heart of every girl since the beginning of time and will be there until the end of time said to me as well: *You are loved, dearly loved by a most noble and extraordinary man, a man who consigns each and every other worshipper and admirer to sorry insignificance.*

Bernhard read my heart, and I did not try to prevent this, but neither did I admit to myself that I was giving him this permission. Instead, I let it happen carelessly, nonchalantly, so to speak. Both of us were now overjoyed, experiencing the first gentle delicate understanding of the fusion of two souls. We certainly felt that we meant something to each other, but we were not ready to express this to the world. First love doesn't always have the words and can in fact dispense with words all together.

Oh, I wish I had remained longer in this state! How differently my life would have turned out. But Princess Mathilde recovered again, and her mother continued her journey and after two weeks that passed by ever so quickly, I went home to my father and to familiar surroundings and way of life.

I felt as though I was awakening from a long lovely dream, but waking up was also pleasant and I did not cry like *Kaliban*[35], to sleep again. Though not exactly painful to me, I was uncomfortable with the separation from my father and the unaccustomed dependency on others. He had business matters to attend to here, as he had stated from the beginning. Bernard von Leuen allowed my father to make introductions as he had already made his acquaintance earlier when he had visited the Princess. From now on, he visited us almost daily.

On my return, our circle of friends and acquaintances received me with loud cheers and treated me like a queen returning to her country after a long absence. Since my absence from home, the atmosphere had not changed in the least. Just as before, our daily agenda included French quips, bold and often unwarranted opinions on every subject, ruthless, malevolent ridiculing of, if not the most sacred, then that which was sacred for many.

Hours could be spent on the most lively discussions about absolutely nothing. Occasionally, men who were better informed, headed by my father, would discuss clearly and sensibly, instructively and thoroughly many of the most important topics concerning life, art and science. The younger ones in our circle silently withdrew from these discussions, only Bernhard always participated with a keen interest. I, on the other hand, took part in all discussions, whether serious or humorous, according to my old habit and often found a special delight in capriciously mixing everything together. Unfortunately, old patterns led the way and with every day memories of the superior, sadly too short time that I spent with the Princess were thrust into the shadow. In my old surroundings, too quickly I had become once more my former self.

Perhaps you may find it incredible, when I tell you that I was secretly pleased when I noticed with a shock how differently I must appear to von Leuen here in my father's house, compared to how I behaved in the presence of the Princess and her environment. But I was foolish and spoiled enough to interpret the visible stir at the moment of discovery, for a sign of astonished admiration. From then on, I became more high-spirited and audacious with each passing day. Next to the joy of receiving my father's applause, I was also carried away by the overzealous admiration of our circle. And of course, I wanted to shine in Bernhard's eyes; to show him how fascinating I was. I spent my days surpassing myself to the highest pitch of my mental faculties, joking with this person, teasing that person, and making decisions often about subjects I could not know about. I would be the first to laugh when gross errors resulted as sometimes happened.

I was not so self-centred that I could ignore the intense sorrow that now clouded Bernhard's fine features. And yet, a few kind words directed to him, some small preferential treatment that I courteously extended to him when he least expected this, never failed to transform his pained expression to one of ardent adoration.

So I believed that his current melancholy was just the effect of jealousy which in my interpretation could only be complimentary. I sensed how he clasped me with heart and soul and I had a childish pleasure in letting him dangle on a silk thread at my whim. I did not think that he would tear himself from this tenuous restraint or find it oppressive; in fact he seemed to wear it gladly. I had no mother, no friend wise and tactful enough, to explain to me just how much this abuse of power was unfair to him and unworthy of me.

Meanwhile, I coupled this strange behaviour, with the intention of making my friend more socially at ease. In my mind, this was all he was missing to be absolutely perfect. In the magnificent and serious atmosphere dominant in the Princess's sphere, I could find no fault with him. But now in my own circle, he often did *not* appear sophisticated enough and sometimes I was inconsolable when I believed that he was being outflanked by less knowledgeable men. After all, I was brilliant and everything that wanted to be a part of my world had to be brilliant as well.

Bernhard seemed reluctant to fulfill my wishes in this respect and unwilling to chase after this illusive lustre that I thought he was missing. He would stay as he had always been and when the dandies dared to come a little too close with their frivolous games, he could be blunt and imposing enough, rising to the occasion to deflect them to a proper distance. This was not exactly what I had in mind, but it did not irk me; in fact I was secretly all the more proud of my friend.

In such instances, Bernhard noticed my approval, though I would hardly have admitted this to myself. This discovery once even gave him the courage to take advantage of the situation to demonstrate to me the pointless and superficial nature of our behaviour.

"How is it possible, dear *Fräulein*," he said to me. "How can you, who are so gifted, find pleasure in the intellectual poverty of these people? How can the pursuits of this society entrance you so? As for myself, please believe me, perhaps I would be deceived about your overindulgence in these trivial quests if my memories were not filled with those glorious first days I experienced near you. I will never forget those days. Let them return. You can do this, as soon as you wish. Just be yourself again!"

"I am always myself," I laughed in response.

"A happy creature that may sometimes be quite serious, but also likes to be amused. And fools just happen to be most amusing."

"Likes to be *amused*," repeated Leuen with some bitterness. "What does that mean? To forget life, chasing one day after the next with lightning speed, playing a game that means nothing and has no purpose? So that no trace remains. So that no one has time to reflect. Oh, *Fräulein*, you could be so happy, just by making others happy," he cried, his face colouring deeply with emotion as he seized my hand.

"Dear Anna, may you always be happy and may all the wonders that life has to offer always be there for you. May all your days be an unbroken chain of joy worthy of you, and . . ." Bernhard paused for a moment then added, "But *amusing* yourself? Dear *Fräulein,* leave that unrelenting intoxication to those who find themselves at about the same level as those whom you allow to flutter around you unnoticed and unappreciated."

"Don't you see, von Leuen," I answered amiably, although I was not entirely satisfied with his response. "Don't you see that in admonishing this innocent amusement, you are highly amusing yourself because you are taking something seriously which is not intended to be taken seriously and that is exactly where the real fun is to be found. Will you never learn to recognize your friends behind the mask?"

"But when they are never without their mask?" he answered.

"It's quite normal during Carnival," I chimed in quickly. "Youth is the carnival of life, after all. You ought to be pleased that you are among the very few in the presence of whom one is glad to air one's mask and that quite often. And now Mr. Faultfinder, come to the piano and accompany me with *Amiets Klagen* from our beloved Kleist. I promise to behave myself for the rest of the evening, unless something happens that could change my mind."

With an expression of love and exasperation in his eyes, an expression that we like to think demonstrates proof of our absolute self-determination, Bernard followed me in docile resignation. Triumphantly I sang: "She flies away, because of me she flies, so great a distance separates me from Lalage."

Almost every day from now on, similar scenes repeated themselves. Often von Leuen was able to recreate them rather artificially. Often I saw the true confession of love trembling on his lips. My heart throbbed in answer to him, but a strange fusion of pride, bashfulness, girlish awkwardness, together with an acute consciousness of my feelings for him, caused me to escape from him in some way each time, even if only by way of a silly jest that promptly popped into my head.

My father's sharp eye did not miss a thing and he was pleased to see how our affection for one another increased day by day. But he did not think it advisable to interfere or encourage us in any way.

At the same time, our social circle was beginning to look upon me as the bride of von Leuen, even though I responded to any such allusions with merely a lofty smile. In any case, I listened to whatever anyone said about this affair, without giving the matter any particular attention.

My future stretched before me limitless and unfathomable and I was happy in the present, the moment was enough for me and I accepted everything as it came, without worry or foresight.

Bernhard grew more serious with each passing day and there were other changes in his behaviour that should have alerted me to his internal conflict but I did not notice it or did not believe it. Then came the fateful evening that decided my future, although unsuspecting, I did not see it coming.

Isn't that how it always is? Like children, we play carelessly at the edge of an abyss, escaping from or even forcefully pushing away the hand that is trying to save us from falling, because at that moment, it cannot help but seizing us a little roughly.

Our usual social circle was larger than normal one evening and the very lively discussion centred around a subject that in those days was a very popular theme among our most fashionable local community. It concerned a young man who had just returned from a sojourn of several years in foreign lands. He had been in Paris for quite some time, and had even spent a few months in Rome and therefore took it upon himself to set the trend to a level of perfection in his home town. Among equals, this was easier to do then than it would be today.

Today the whole world goes on jaunts and we are less impressed by those worldly individuals whom we considered more awe-inspiring in my time. Anyone who had seen Paris, that generally acknowledged queen of all cities, automatically had a huge advantage in society on that basis alone. And someone who had also been to Rome, and could say something about the Pope's slippers! Well, he would be regarded with a kind of shy reverence, as if he had undertaken and accomplished something monumental.

This young Wiesenau, for that was the name of this well-travelled individual, was the perfect example of his kind and aroused the prejudice of his contemporaries. In our social circle, nothing found grace in his eyes. He condemned everything, calling it ridiculous or pitiful, whether he was referring to carriages, house-hold utensils, clothing or hair styles. But he was incessant and indomitable in showing off the latest Paris fashions, relating each detail to the utmost degree without tiring himself in the least. All the young gentlemen in our group were becoming exasperated because despite every possible effort of their craftsmen, working night and day, still they were unable to duplicate Wiesenau's creations. The king of fashion was more despotic thirty or forty years than today and anyone who deviated ever so slightly from the latest fashion rules in his set, could hardly allow himself to be seen, if he had not already dispensed with elegance and novelty.

Obviously, this cosmopolitan wonder caused quite a sensation among the ladies as well. Delighted was the lady able to engage in conversation with Herr von Wiesenau and happier still was she who knew how to captivate that chimerical butterfly for a few hours. The most ecstatic were the few who had aroused much envy because he had provided them with large Parisian fashion dolls complete with assorted ensembles. In those days, such fashion dolls would be sent from Paris to prominent families in Europe. Those selected by von Wiesenau would use these models to completely transform themselves almost beyond recognition from head to toe.

Incidentally, this young man was not merely considered the epitome of elegant fashion, he was also admired as the most amusing, charming and refined *petit-maître* that one had seen in at least fifty years. Everyone echoed his most entertaining anecdotes. Only von Leuen, who had met him abroad was not quite in accordance with this choir of admirers. Von Leuen proclaimed him to be a common, brazen dandy and further elaborated that in fact von Wiesenau himself had often been the butt of jokes. Moreover, he was only capable of cranking out memorized refrains in an ape-like manner.

In retrospect, I still felt rather neutral towards this hero of the day, since I had not yet met him. Since I was not interested in his fashion dolls, I was not nearly as impressed with him as the other members of our group. After everything I had heard about him and because I generally liked to play devil's advocate, I was more inclined to take the side of von Leuen. However, von Wiesenau was more popular at the moment and he was brilliant, no one could deny this, so I decided I would allow him to tag along a little in my victory chariot as soon as the opportunity presented itself. I had the opportunity even before I expected it, that very evening when one of our house-guests brought this extensively discussed individual to us for a visit.

My dear children, you can only imagine what a dandy actually looked like in our day; the theatre only gives you a very general idea since this look is now *passé,* thank goodness. I wish posterity well with this loss, although I don't necessarily want to praise something which has become an object of ridicule, I must say that the foolishness of today is less humiliating if not as prevalent. I could hardly contain myself, as this preposterous, contrived and perfumed figure of idolatry on bended knee first kissed my hand while his pigeon wings powdered *à la Maréchal* brushed close to my knees. I had never seen such a caricature before in my life.

The little man had learned to palaver in Paris and revealed some rather original ideas. He possessed a haughty superficial bantering tone to boot; one that showed no mercy and I knew exactly how to respond to him. The two of us led the conversation that evening and the rest of the group was contented themselves with applauding or laughter in measured intervals.

The conversation soon took a turn in a direction quite hateful to my friend and I could not prevent it. But in my impudence I did not stop. Instead, I competed with the newcomer in ruthlessly mocking everything that the French connoisseurs called prejudice, as a result of the modern enlightenment of the time. Absent members of our group were not spared from the sting of our arrows.

Please excuse me, my darlings, if I don't give you the details of a conversation that would hurt me deeply if I were to repeat it to you. I would prefer to forget it, but until this moment I have not succeeded in wiping it from my memory.

The eager attention of our audience, interrupted now and then with shrieks of laughter, was reward enough for our efforts. Even my father, smiling good-naturedly listened to us, while Bernhard became ever more silent and serious. I saw the restrained indignation blazing in his dark eyes and read the quiet pain in his expression regarding my behaviour, but it did not occur to me to spare him because of this. In spite of his unhappiness, my foolish vanity lead me to defy exactly that which was causing his unhappiness. My defiance continued to the point that he could no longer tolerate it.

I sat in a corner near the fireplace and I was partially hidden from the guests who formed a semi-circle across from me by the fireplace screen and a little table that stood by my side. Meanwhile, almost unnoticed, Bernhard found his way to my armchair. Behind me, bending over the back of the chair, he whispered a plea that I should stop this mischievous entertainment. All in vain! Instead, I looked as though I did not understand him at all.

Now his pleas became more urgent and turned into warnings. Zealous with the fervour of passion and indignation, he finally (without actually wanting to) mingled the long delayed confession of intimate love with a desperate plea that I return to myself and my better nature.

This moment was the supreme triumph of my life. I had achieved something, something that I could never have dreamed, not in my wildest imagination. He, Bernhard von Leuen had to swallow his pride, right in the middle of his frustration over my behaviour. He had to acknowledge my victory. And yet the warm love in my heart surged towards him and at that moment I would have given the world to be able to confess everything I thought and felt to him in privacy. Still, I was driven by an irresistible arrogance, a demonic lust for his suffering, and to continue with this hateful game. I was aware that I could on a whim turn anguish into charm.

Too excited to fully understand what I was doing, I appeared to be more brilliant than ever with my inexhaustible supply of wit. Bernhard just stood there, silent and pale. No good angel counselled me to stop while there was still time. It seems as though I fell prey to the dark forces of doom as punishment for my haughtiness. You would almost believe that they control these little equally unexpected and destructive coincidences that enter our lives.

Certainly it was just such a coincidence. I still don't know how it happened that our fanciful arrows turned toward Bernhard. Transfixed by my behaviour, some thoughtless words he flung in my direction may have been the first, though not intended cause of what ensued. He was simply too agitated, too offended in the deepest recesses of his mind to be capable of returning the attack of his opponent. This bitter game disgusted his good nature too much, to be able to successfully participate.

Of course he tried to defend himself but he confused himself in the attempt and for once did not find the right words for what he wanted to say. I saw this and his confusion heightened my sense of triumph. Swept up by the jubilation, I was reckless enough to reclaim one of his expressions and ridiculed it.

Bernhard looked at me, dazed with bewilderment. I will never forget the expression on his face.

Suddenly there was a conspicuous and embarrassing silence around me. I believed that everyone wanted to spare me through him. I forgot that probably no one there would really want to continue this ridiculing of someone who was so often envied, whose intellectual superiority each of them had experienced often enough but I did not shy away. I looked up and my evil demon showed me how across from me everyone wore a sly triumphant smile. He alone stood there, robbed of his usual weapon, in the middle of this, to me, unbelievably hateful crowd. They pretended to want to spare him out of pity.

Now because of him, I began to suffer terribly. At this despicable moment, I felt so ashamed and for the first time, I realized what he meant to me and my boundless love for him. In abysmal confusion, an anguish beyond words, I was simultaneously high-spirited and humiliated, completely unsettled by an inexplicable dark power bordering on despair.

Still I had to say a few words. Wild, uncontrollable laughter followed my words and it pained me to hear the shrill cutting tone of this laughter because it was directed at my dear friend, whom I loved with an almost delirious passion. And I had exposed him to the derision of these people.

Bernhard stood up and suddenly everything was silent again. He walked towards me, looked straight into my eyes, took hold of my hand and kissed it. Without saying another word, he left our circle. A deathly silence filled the room.

The pain crushed me now with devastating violence; I was completely overcome with emotion. I would have said that my entire life stood still. Every beat of my heart seemed to say, "You have lost him, you and him, forever, you are to blame."

Angelika! Victorine! Have you ever felt this kind of pain?

I no longer knew what I was doing. Mechanically, I seized a small, but very lovely porcelain potpourri vase that had been placed on the small table beside me. It slid through my hands. Was it clumsiness? Or did I instinctively let it drop, to draw attention away from myself. I was never really sure about this. The latter was at least the apparent aftermath, and the group seemed to experience a glimmering perception about the harm that had just occurred. They were therefore all quite happy, to focus their attention elsewhere.

My pallor, my tremulous swaying, now seemed to have a visible cause and the group was fortunately able to escape from the silent embarrassment vexing them until now. The vase painted with the Cupid figure now lay at shattered at my feet, and the regret over its destruction sparked countless spirited remarks and witty observations. Despite the silliness of it all, many of these cut deep into my heart.

However, this incident, though partly coincidental, triggered a change in the conversation and I was forced to take control of myself for the rest of this shameful evening."

CHAPTER 12

"I think this is enough for today!" said the aunt quietly as she slowly lifted herself from the armchair. The girls had been crying and the aunt kissed them both on the forehead, her bright eyes soulful and full of meaning gazed at the two of them for some time. She looked as though she wanted to say something else, but her voice failed her. Gently she turned around and left the room, signalling that they should not follow her. She did not appear again that evening.

As she had always done for so many years, Anna von Falkenhayn sat fully dressed in her armchair at seven o'clock the next morning, although in the Kleeborn household all was quiet, just as it was in the other larger houses in the city.

Her eyes were sad; her heart was heavy with the weight of a thousand tender and sorrowful memories. Her face, supported by her delicate transparent hand, looked almost colourless. For a long time she had been trying in vain to focus her attention on the open book in front of her. She thought that this would finally help to diminish the echo of misty joyful hours that she had re-awakened the evening before.

So when her maid announced that someone unfamiliar to her needed to see her urgently, the unexpected distraction was not altogether agreeable. She was all the more reluctant to receive this visitor, as the maid had not been successful in obtaining a name.

"The young man," she said, "looks so distinguished that I found it difficult to ask for his name." Feeling annoyed and out of sorts, Anna von Falkenhayn was ready to convey to the somewhat inconvenient stranger that his visit would be better postponed to a more agreeable time. Then suddenly the thought came to her that precisely this unusual visiting hour may be signalling something more than a customary visit, so rather than submit to a mood and thereby possibly lose an opportunity to be helpful to someone, she gave him permission to enter.

As he made his way into the room Anna experienced a sense of alarm, though she could not understand why. She recognized him immediately as the Victorine's lover.

Although Anna was at least twice the age of the young man, both were flushed and appeared to be strangely embarrassed. But this odd self-consciousness did not last long. Anna was too self-possessed to succumb to the situation and after a few minutes Raimund and Anna sat across from each other completely at ease, like a pair of old acquaintances.

Raimund excused himself for his unconventionally early visit, although prior to coming he had ensured through his old friend Müller that for this distinguished lady, the day began at least two hours earlier than in the rest of the house. However he was determined not to disturb her and if possible remain unnoticed.

A little flustered now, he wanted to try to proceed with his actual matter of concern, but Anna obliged him by revealing that she had already gained Victorine's confidence, and had been initiated into the hidden mysteries of their love. So the conversation between the two was soon free of any cumbersome restrictions and they were now able to speak about what was nearest to their heart, without further constraint.

Finding courage from her graceful tranquillity, Raimund now explained to the aunt how a proposition from Herr Fischer, which he would neither accept or reject without Victorine's approval, was the main motive behind seeking her advice. Herr Fischer's proposal concerned a long, potentially dangerous sea voyage, the undertaking of which would lead to the possibility of personally directing a promising enterprise in a foreign country. Upon his hopefully happy return, he would be rewarded for his efforts with a significant share in this respected enterprise.

"As soon as I had gotten over my first angry reaction towards Herr Kleeborn's behaviour," Raimund added after explaining to her the anticipated dangers as well as the advantages of this undertaking.

"As soon as I had overcome my initial resentment, in other words as soon as I had come back to my senses, that's all it took for me to come to a decision. With consideration to any failures at the start, once the path was taken, I was determined to stay on the course. Should we accept that we are simply in a game of chance? Groping blindly, sometimes holding on, sometimes letting go, driven by whim? Shouldn't we hold fast to the decisions we have made, to at least save that never recurring episode from the shipwreck of our dreams?"

"I am happy that you have such strong convictions," answered Aunt Anna. "For even Victorine . . ."

"Oh, certainly!" interrupted Raimund. "I know my Victorine and the shadow of doubt will never diminish my view of this noble creature. I know that Victorine will remain faithful to me, no matter how much Herr Kleeborn may want to force this stranger upon her, he will never win her hand. But she will never belong to me either, as long as her father is alive to forbid it, for she is just as true to her sense of duty as she is to love. And so probably for a long period of mourning, the two of us are destined to yearn in unfulfilled desire, unless a good angel changes our fate to something happier. How this might happen, this foolish man is not able to see yet," sighed Raimund with a sad expression.

Anna von Falkenhayn, seemed destined to be a gentle consoler to everyone who came to her and she was happy to try to advise her new young friend, and especially to reconcile his life with his own potential. Meanwhile, much had to be seriously weighed and considered before making a firm decision concerning the suggested trip. For this reason Raimund continued to visit the aunt early in the morning. Her charm and just being around her intrigued him. He felt irresistibly drawn to this unusual woman who was a lifeline, the link between himself and Victorine.

When Anna spoke to him so kindly, it made him think of his father. Since he had lost his father, no one spoke to him this way. Most of all, he was filled with a sweet, almost unearthly melancholy, and now looking at the ageing features of her pale serious face, he noticed an unmistakable similarity between her and his magnificent beloved, who was in the splendid bloom of youth.

Then it seemed to him that the dark veil of the future was lifted, gazing soberly and secretively at him, while the crushing weight of time enveloped him, with a resounding warning to hold on to youth, before it disappears forever.

The young man grew dearer to the aunt as well, the more she saw of him, but not because she learned to understand him better. You might say, she judged him as women generally judge men; with the heart and not with the mind. For someone with her intelligence, this was unusual. Everything about him, his manner, his way of speaking, his behaviour; everything appeared to be an accompaniment to the melody of her most inner being and thus already most familiar to her.

"Finally, my dear friend and supporter, finally I must come to a decision regarding my journey," Raimund wrote the aunt on the morning when he was detained from visiting her. "I am pressured by time," he continued "and I can no longer legitimately excuse myself from giving my well-wishing friends a proper decision. I spent the quiet of the night to thoroughly examine everything once again. Herr Fischer's offer provides me with an opportunity for a completely independent, perhaps even bright future, that I may offer Victorine, at least after her father has passed away, even if he decides to completely disinherit her upon our marriage. Perhaps he will now be less obstinate about this union with the son of a business associate when he learns that I am far away. And likely Victorine will be more able to break away from the hold that her father has on her. I am not worried about my personal welfare in any case, because Victorine's prayers will protect me from any possible human or elemental dangers.

So, dear lady, I only ask you to bring me Victorine's permission to go. And this as soon as possible. The sooner I go, the sooner I can return. And who knows, perhaps while I am away, the guiding spirit of our love will find a happy solution for us."

CHAPTER 13

Although he did not oppose the reasoning of her young friend, it was only with inner reluctance that she undertook to fulfil Raimund's wish. She was a little alarmed, when Victorine, far more collected and composed than she had expected, consented to let her beloved go. Actually, it was Victorine's lively spirit that amplified her misfortune, the distressing feeling of being inextricably so close and yet so far away from her beloved. It had become almost unbearable to her that any change in their situation must, on the other hand, appear to her like a victory.

Her passionate fantasy, always striving for the future, could find nothing in the everyday life of a man of business on which to pin her hopes, especially since he was not permitted to approach her. Where should she look for him? At the stock exchange? Working at his desk? Through his daily contact with the business world, or with his assistants?

"No, Aunt!" cried Victorine. "Let him go. My blessing, my prayers, my dreams will accompany him everywhere, always. It isn't like before, when I believed that he wanted to flee to Odessa forever from an exaggerated sense of noble-mindedness. He's leaving, that's true, but he isn't leaving me. He's going where his duty calls him, but he is leaving so that he may possibly return happier than when he left. In our situation, it doesn't matter whether it's a distance of a thousand miles or a thousand steps. To me, it will seem like Raimund is closer somehow. I would rather imagine him under a starry deep blue southern sky, standing on the deck of his ship as it is cutting through powerful waves. Far better that my spirit pursues him in the shuffle of arrival in or departure from foreign cities, than to seek him here, in the vast colourless, amorphous wasteland of everyday life, which is nothing more than a blur to me."

With her usual perseverance, Victorine made only one more request and Raimund agreed with her immediately when he heard what it was. She asked to be able to see him, with her father's permission and her aunt's watchful eyes, for one hour, before his departure.

This aunt, this gentle spirit who protected her niece's life and love, now tried in vain to persuade the lovers to spare her from this last bittersweet hour. Not only was she overruled, but the two lovers also requested that she obtain Herr Kleeborn's permission for this meeting. Somehow, Raimund's eloquence exerted an irresistible power over her.

"Don't force me," he asked her. "Don't force me to run away from pain like a coward. It's against my nature to shirk or run away; it's abhorrent to me. Whatever happens to me, I want to look adversity straight in the eyes, even if it means my ruin. Many people wish for a quick death . . . since my childhood I have shunned death. If I have to die, I want to die fully aware of what is about to occur, so that my fading eyes can gaze thankfully one last time at the sun and stars that have lighted the way for me so long. So even now, before I go, perhaps never to return, I want to look in Victorine's devoted eyes once more . . . in the sunlight of a brighter life. Who knows if they will light my way again, because my journey is far and many dangers threaten to bring harm to me."

"The young Holm is on his way to England and from there to the West Indies, this is certain," the aunt said to Herr Kleeborn, trying to sound as neutral as was possible for her in this situation. Actually, she was simply hoping to start a conversation with him in this manner, a way to fulfil her promise, without creating more awkwardness for herself.

But Kleeborn was visibly shaken when he heard this name mentioned so calmly, a name that until now he would not have had the courage to say out loud in her presence. In speechless amazement, he gazed at her, thereby prompting her to repeat her comment.

"Holm!" he cried almost exultation. "The young Holm from Fisher and Company? Well, *bon voyage*! Well, dear sister. You couldn't have brought me better news. Even if you had told me that I had won the largest share in the English lottery! Nothing is more important to me than the domestic peace and happiness of my only child. What an intelligent woman you are! Well, of course, I've always thought and said that you are a woman who knows the world. There I was, racking my brain about how to break this confounded story to you in a reasonable manner so that you would know exactly what I mean. And in the meantime you have silently assimilated all the details, controlled the situation and brought everything to an excellent conclusion. Well, well! I think everything will be settled with time. But first this bone of contention must be dealt with. Victorine will be more reasonable, when you . . ."

The aunt interrupted him so that she would not have to hear more than necessary.

CHAPTER 14

"I have permitted Herr Holm to say goodbye to Victorine in my presence," she said with steady composure and the same impartiality as before. Herr Kleeborn was a little bewildered and did not know how to answer her. She spoke with such absolute certitude, as if it could not be otherwise, and her respectful restraint virtually barred any possible contradiction, especially since she had just brought him such good news.

Still, he was very reluctant to give his explicit consent to the meeting of the two lovers, even though he was certain it would be their last. After a moment's thought, he found a compromise, by simply acting as if he hadn't heard Anna's last words.

"All's well that ends well, once is enough," he muttered to himself. After a short pause, he realized that his sister-in-law didn't think it was a good idea to add anything more to the discussion, because this would have given him opportunity to challenge her, so without further hesitation, he left the room to go to his office.

Anna was happy about this little triumph; it was fair enough and she had not asked for more than what was necessary. She believed that this mute consent was quite satisfactory and she would be able to use it without misgiving.

Finally, the morning of Raimund's departure arrived and the two lovers met, as had been their wish. But what a reunion! Reconciliation and separation, heavenly bliss and a sorrow beyond words converged on the apex of a single moment. The first impulse of life and the chill of death almost fused in the ephemeral suspension of the hour.

Happy and melancholy, wordless and yet infinitely eloquent, Raimund and Victorine, held captive in their embrace until the hour of separation sounded. The aunt heard the toll of the bell confirming the hour. Lost in her own thoughts, she had been sitting there all the while. She stood up now and looked first at Raimund. Breaking through the clouds, a faint ray of sunlight dramatized the sad expression on his gentle face.

Anna shuddered as if suddenly seized by a violent pain and her hand twitched involuntarily towards her heart, her eyes fixed vaguely on Raimund's somber expression. A painful cry escaped from deep within her, turning pale, she swayed and looked as if she were about to faint. Alarmed, Victorine and Raimund rushed to her assistance to guide her to the sofa, but Anna recovered amid a stream of tears that seemed to pacify her anxious heart.

Now Raimund pressed the joined hands once more to his feverish lips, these two that were so dear to him. Then he hurried away. They watched as the beloved figure disappeared through the door, this man who would not walk through that door again for a long time. Perhaps he never would again.

They could hear the sound of Raimund's footsteps, as he walked along the lengthy corridor. Weaker and weaker came the sound, until the distance was too great. Silently, Victorine listened until the sound faded away completely, then she flung herself into Anna's open arms, that faithful soul who seemed to be struggling with a sorrow as intense as her own.

The imaginary terror of her beloved's dangerous journey that had almost frightened Victorine to death was now a reality. It is said that the Persians believe that every spoken word is transformed into a spirit that wanders the earth ceaselessly until it reaches the gates of paradise, where it takes form.

It was curious how Victorine was able to endure this very real pain with more composure than had been expected. Fully aware of, and resigned to her situation, she still cherished Anna's tender support. Out of Victorine's sacrifice today surged hope for a happier future; then lulled to rest the almost impatient yearning that had gripped her too often in the lonely hours.

Her physical condition no longer required special care, but her spirit required a tranquil harbour and she found this shelter only with the aunt and Angelika.

Babet and Agathe were now permitted to visit their friends more frequently in the still quiet hours of the evening, but as soon as the occasion arose and urged by her dear nieces, Anna continued the thread of her life story.

As much as possible, her story will be told in her own words, leaving out the comments of her listeners, as well as occasional interruptions and pauses.

CHAPTER 15

Continuation of Anna's life story

"A black unyielding and impenetrable gloom weighed upon me, after that desperate evening," said Anna von Falkenhayn as she continued with her story.

"It seemed as though my grief would never end, my eyes were dry and feverish, rigid with a dark despair that no star could illuminate. I could not even close them for a moment to induce a comforting temporary amnesia.

That first sleepless night I was tortured by remorse and the grim shadow of self-reproach has remained my entire life. Since then, countless troubled nights followed, though thank God, none were quite as hopeless as that night. I was never quite so devastated again.

In vain I tried to salvage my pride, to find new courage. In vain I wanted to scold this foolish woman, to lighten my burden, this burden that threatened to crush me. My heart professed the most ardent love, but each beat intensified the bitter remorse that bordered on self-contempt and I struggled to maintain my former vain assurance.

Finally morning came. At any rate, morning brings even the most unhappy creature a little courage and consolation, however brief. I began to hope that Bernhard could not be separated from me forever in this way. At least, I still cherished the hope that this was so.

I got up and tried as quickly as possible to free myself from this nocturnal dread, but when I looked at the mirror I was alarmed when I saw the pale, ghostly and overwrought face stare back at me. For the first time in my life I was forced to practise those little cosmetic arts, which I had always treated with contempt. I was most determined to approach the man I loved openly and honestly, open my heart unconditionally to him and if necessary I was ready to yield to a confession of my arrogant folly. However I did not want Bernhard to see too clearly what had transpired by looking at my face.

These thoughts preoccupied me for most of the morning and I deluded myself by lingering as long as possible on my contemplations. Later on, I did everything I could just to avoid seeing how late it was and that the hour when Bernhard usually came to visit me was already long gone. My poor heart was pounding hard and fast.

Finally, someone brought me a farewell card with Bernhard's name on it. My father was given a sealed envelope containing Bernhard's general expression of thanks for all previously rendered kindness, though he did not mention the destination of his journey.

My father avoided looking at me, but after reading Bernhard's message, he handed me the envelope. Never before had I felt so hurt and forlorn.

Soon after, I excused myself with the not entirely contrived pretext of feeling unwell and left for my own room, where I remained in seclusion for a number of days. I really needed to do this just so that I could think about my situation. I needed to get away! That was my main intention.

It would be impossible for me to see the same company, where I would miss Bernhard. But where could I go? I had no friends, not even a female acquaintance who could grant me protection and shelter in this awkward situation. They had all escaped from the blinding dazzle of the vanity that had surrounded me until then.

At first I thought of going to the Duchess von P. At our last parting, she had honoured me with an invitation for an undetermined time, but who knows, perhaps Bernhard with his wounded heart had already flown to her? In this case, was it proper, or even sensible to invite suspicion? As if I had purposely followed him? And supposing that everything would be the same as usual, only without him. How would I be able to endure that? The questions that people would ask? How could I talk about him, every hour, every day? To hear him being praised, without giving way to despair?

The more I thought about my situation, the more hopeless everything seemed to me and I began to feel very sorry for myself. I could not continue to live as I had until now. This was very clear to me. Our usual tasteless carrying-on had driven Bernhard away and disgusted me now beyond words, but how could I leave without appearing foolish? To me, this seemed a fate worse than death. How could I ask my dear father to give up old friendships and familiar habits on my account?

I could not see a way out and I exhausted myself with futile contemplation about how I could leave a world that until a few days ago had been the stage for my triumphs. What had once seemed essential to me was now most detestable to me.

My health would likely have been adversely affected if this situation had lasted longer, but like an unexpected messenger of peace sent from Heaven, a letter came for me and my anxiety disappeared.

If I had received this letter just a few days ago, I would have been inconsolable; I was now captivated by the letter. It contained none other than a request from the provost of my college asking that I resume my studies which had been postponed for too long. Since coming of age, I was obliged to spend at least a few months each year at the college. This guaranteed that there would not be any further delay in the fulfilment of my obligations, since it had already been too long.

Hardly able to suppress my excitement, I told my father the news and my decision to meet my commitment as soon as possible. My dear father did not object and in fact he made haste to take care of all the necessary details for my quick departure.

But he was so quiet, and looked so sad that I was deeply affected. His eyes and his attitude towards me revealed that he had not only guessed what I had experienced, but that he also had anxious doubts about whether the excellent education he had provided was an adequate foundation for my true happiness.

This concern, which came too late in any case, visibly affected him. When a plan doesn't succeed, few people are strong enough to consider only the good intention or purpose, rather than the outcome. We ought not to forget that we should comfort ourselves for having aimed for the best, even when the joy of success has been denied us.

I felt as happy as if I were escaping from prison. Finally, on this dreary autumn morning, I was leaving my father's home with my sorrows, to seek solitude in unfamiliar surroundings. My father had requested that my sister Karoline, who was twelve years old at this time, would accompany me on this journey.

Our trip would take us through a rich, lush and fertile region but this could not be fully appreciated by a young girl, because the budding green buoyancy of spring was lacking. Now, in late autumn the cold biting wind cut across the fields of brush and whipped through the sparse yellow foliage of the trees. Everything that I looked at seemed gloomy and lifeless to me, without the slightest trace of the past beauty.

Unable to hide her apprehension, poor little Karoline clung tightly to me, as we approached the dark low curve of the gate by nightfall. This was the entrance to a former convent and now provided accommodation for the sisters.

I shuddered a little as we shuffled in semi-darkness through the long cloister. At the far end were the rooms reserved for me.

We passed by many low archways that seemed to lead to the former living quarters. While walking by, I heard loud female voices, as if a violent quarrel were taking place among the general commotion of chirping canaries, the hoarse barking of pugs, interrupted by the cantankerous shrieking of cockatoos and parrots.

More frightened than before, Karoline held on to my arm and even our maidservant kept as close as possible to us, looking quite intimidated as she peered into every corner.

A door opened. It appeared to be quite similar to those we had passed. We faced the sitting room, where at this moment the evening sun already below the horizon was piercing through the heavy grey cloud cover that had veiled the sun all day. Through the purple-red leaves of the wild vines that twisted around the window, the sun cheerfully shone on our faces. The bouncing shadows of branches played merrily on the pale green wall. Everything looked so comfortable and welcoming that we embraced the refreshing ray of sunshine as a good omen.

The little room was large enough for us; it could easily be furnished to make it quite cozy and comfortable. With great enthusiasm, Karoline and our maidservant immediately occupied themselves with unpacking and arranging our belongings, as if we were going to settle here for an entire lifetime. In the meantime, I looked for a quiet corner where I could immerse myself without being disturbed.

My solitude for the next few months was actually reclusive; an almost violent contrast to my former life. At first, I felt that oppressive pursuit of contemplation, like a fear that shadows us after surviving some great danger. But by and by I was more at peace with myself and was able to see more clearly. With the sincere desire to be not only true but also fair to myself, I examined my past as well as my future, attempting to draw the most logical conclusions from this present impasse of my life.

I was already convinced at that time that neither time nor force of circumstances could ever tear Bernhard from my heart. He would live there from now on, as if in a quiet sanctuary. The more clearly I saw the wrong that I had shamelessly inflicted on both of us, the more my efforts and attention focused on my deeply wounded friend, and the more firmly I made up my mind to make amends, so that I would be worthy of him.

I promised myself that he would be a part of my life, even if I should never see him again. Everything else I would leave to fate. Secretly, and quietly I still hoped that a lucky star, or perhaps his own heart would lead him back to me. And then . . . well, I didn't dare to think further than that.

For the most part, in these surroundings, I was left to myself. Several hours of the day I would regularly dedicate for Karoline's lessons. The rest of the time, that compliant child would spend mostly with a family in the neighbourhood, where she not only found playmates of her age but also learned to know about and love the quiet domesticity of family life. Almost always, I stayed alone in my room.

With the approach of winter, the younger sisters were away, intending to stay with their relatives. The remaining older sisters did not pay that much attention to me. As soon as the initial curiosity about my sudden and unexpected arrival had been satisfied, they returned to their customary pleasures such as socializing over coffee, or playing *Trißett* and *l'Hombre*[36]. They did not take it amiss that I showed little interest in participating in these games.

In the end, my contact in the convent was restricted to mainly the provost, the Countess von ***, who belonged to one of the oldest and most noble families in Germany. But her inner nobility elevated her far above her inherited rank and position. She had been chained to this refuge for many years by an incurable painful condition that was slowly consuming her.

I was sympathetic at first to her painful suffering, but as I got to know her better, her true Christian humility, her devout submission to the will of God, her almost joyful acceptance of everything meted out to her, my deepest admiration and compassion were awakened. I was also very happy to seek her affection and I hoped that she would want to have my company whenever she had an hour without pain.

Her conversation, the books that I read to her, which were for the most part religious in nature, and most of all the genuine devotion and childlike trust in God she exhibited, all had the most beneficial influence on me, in almost the same way as with my earlier short acquaintance with the Duchess von P., who had had such an impact on the development of my mind.

I will never be able to adequately acknowledge the guiding hand that directed me, leading me to these two noble women at just the right moment in my life. In some respects, one perfected what the other had begun, and for everything that I became later, for all that gave me comfort and light in this labyrinth of life, I thank them both.

It is said that misery seeks company and soon my newly acquired aristocratic friend sensed that I too was not happy, even though I permitted myself a complaint as rarely as she permitted herself a question.

Her own pain made her perceptive enough to read my heart like an open book and with her long years of experience, true motherly concern, and her quiet mild touch, she directed me to that light sent from heaven, a light which seemed to brighten the night of her own suffering. From her, I learned to believe and hope, even though every earthly comfort and happiness disintegrates before our eyes.

With an enriched mind and raised consciousness, and arduously acquired but now stronger backbone, and with my resolution not to allow myself to yield to pretension and deception, after eight months I finally left this solitude that had become so precious to me. I hurried back to my father, whose uncertain health required the care of his children more than ever.

Other than my preoccupation with taking care of and keeping that venerable old man in good spirits, whom I unfortunately found in a much worse condition than I had anticipated, my chief concern was Karoline's further education.

More beautiful day by day, from the bud of childhood the lovely potent bloom of youth burst forth. The sight of Karoline delighted not only her father but everyone who came her way.

To my great relief I discovered that a significant change had taken place in our household during my absence. His advancing ill-health and the lack of a mistress of the household to manage family matters had made it impossible for my father to preserve the large social circle that used to gather in our home.

The group had gradually dissolved all on its own, with the exception of a few of our older friends. In its place a smaller selected collection of friends met likewise with my father every evening. This had been his habit since youth; it would have been impossible to give up these social evenings entirely now that he was an old man.

The conversations of these little *soirées* was certainly very different from the prevailing fashionable brilliance of former times, but I had also become a completely different person in the meantime. So I was quite satisfied to lead a different sort of life.

Every vacuum in my present existence was filled with thoughts of my hopefully not lost forever friend. Often I would wake myself up from pleasant dreams of a happier time, where I hoped to compensate us both for everything that we had suffered through my own fault. Admittedly, I was not able to see what unforeseen opportunity could be precipitated, but I lost myself once again in the realm of possibilities.

Meanwhile, my complete ignorance of Bernhard's whereabouts and how he was managing began to grieve me more and more each day. Since he left us, it seemed as though he had been whisked away from the earth and I would never hear even his name mentioned again. I was tongue-tied by with a natural hesitation that prevented me from asking about him. But even my father mentioned him so rarely, almost as if he had never known him. Partly this was because he probably wanted to spare me, but perhaps more so out of annoyance over the two of us.

Although the number of our daily visitors was sharply limited, our house was open and hospitable to travellers just as before. My father's vast number of diverse foreign contacts often sent us travellers from distant regions, so that almost daily we received some very interesting company. Their fleeting presence injected our monotonous domesticity with a little diversion and variation.

One evening, about a year since Bernhard had left us, by coincidence several visitors had gathered in our home and some of them knew how to quickly liven up the discussion with their conversational skills. One in particular, with his clipped manner of speaking appeared to be exclusively chasing paradoxes. By asserting these, he astonished and impressed if not the world, at least those who were listening to him. In spite of this, all in all, this combative hero was far less unpleasant and annoying than one would believe from this description.

He did not seem to be malicious, but had every word in his power. Occasionally he demonstrated a good deal of wit and humour but if his claims were perceived as excessive he was nimble enough to immediately reveal that he had not really been serious. It was obvious that it was the commotion and excitement that stimulated his figures of speech. He was like a child trying to imitate the beat of a drum by shouting senselessly, so it was impossible to be angry with him, although he sometimes made things rather difficult.

I don't know how it happened, but towards the end of the evening the conversation finally turned to wonderfully articulate and meaningful plots, whereby almost everyone present contributed, for the most part in a loquacious flurry.

Nothing is more contagious and simultaneously short-lived as this desire to tell stories and as soon as the tone is set even by just one person, it is generally embraced by all. By the same token, nothing is rarer than the gift of being able to present a good story well.

On this particular evening, we had many occasions to confirm these observations. Finally, came the turn of one of the most unyielding of story-tellers, a story-teller who is never able to come to the end of the story. Every word is only a repetition of what came before, an effort to improve on what has already been said.

Our quarrelsome stranger, I will call him Lothario because I never learned his true name, let this colossal maelstrom of magnanimity, gratitude and generosity go by in relative tranquillity. But finally his patience ran out, compounded by distinct signs of weariness and boredom in our faces. He jumped up.

"Stop," he cried in an almost piteous tone of voice while he folded his hands in a most curious way. "Stop, for God's sake, stop! Stop all this nonsense about your cursed virtues, that by the light of day are nothing more than affectation, vanity and likely even injustice. You can practise these on yourselves!"

"Everyone always strives to be fair to oneself and to others, before learning how to practise generosity," Lothario added in a very serious tone of voice.

"What we call generosity is usually arrogance in disguise. But being fair or just is really a fundamental duty. And those who seriously subscribe to practising it everywhere *perfectly* will likely have to meet with their fathers a long time before, prior to obtaining permission to be generous."

"Don't tell me about *gratitude*," Lothario exclaimed a little too loudly when several voices conveyed their opposition using that word.

"Gratitude is simply a bad habit, nothing more," he continued. "Actually, under certain circumstances you might call it a burden. At the very least, those who demand gratitude are dealers in slavery, if we don't want to compare them to something worse. Believing they are doing something good, at least their own conception of what *good* is, they attempt to buy the soul of someone for all eternity with a miserable favour or a few measly pieces of gold. But someone who feels an interminable debt of gratitude because someone else rescued him from a fire is at the very least a simpleton, and I am trying to be polite here. Why? Because he doesn't realize that the compensation for such actions is simply the satisfaction of having accomplished a good and honest deed."

Lothario's words made an inexpressibly sad impression upon me because they vividly reminded me of a time where I too would express and fervently defend similar opinions pieced together out of truth and deception just so I would appear brilliant. I could only look back on those days with bitterness.

In the meantime, almost everyone rose against him and he had his hands full defending himself against his attackers. Although it never really degenerated into something distasteful or abusive, this dispute did become ever more boisterous and spirited. Finally, they settled on the proposition that all had challenged and Lothario had deftly asserted: that it is just as wrong and unfair to sacrifice one's own happiness for the benefit of others as it is to treat others preferentially for self-gain.

"Well, then!" cried Lothario conclusively. His voice was in jeopardy of being drowned out in the ever increasing outburst of noise.

"Come, now, I'd like to have a word! Almost all of you have had the chance to tell your stories, so let me tell mine. Allow me to present you with a single example which will illustrate my contention, because it seems to me that I am not being understood. The young lady here can settle the dispute; in difficult cases I always defer to the unfailing instinct of women. They know what's right and wrong without having to brood about it too much, because they sense it."

"Once upon a time," began Lothario as everyone became quiet in order to listen to him, "once there was a young man, healthy in mind and body, well-taught and intelligent and unspoiled by the world's distractions and yet acquainted enough with these, so he did not yearn for them. Enough; here was a man, obliged as the oldest son to restore the long-neglected fairly extensive family estate that was now in a state of decline.

Until now, family concerns and various other matters prevented this major son from troubling himself about his property. Finally, though, after an absence of many years and extensive travelling, he arrived unexpectedly at the family castle. His intention was to improve the pitiful conditions of his farmers and to devote himself to his own equally neglected possessions.

Completely taken by surprise, he encounters his only brother who is several years younger. Oddly enough, he hardly knew him since until now, there had been no contact between them.

This young man, who had just come of age, had left his previous residence, simply to seek the help and guidance of his older brother. He was the son of their father's second wife, from whom he had divorced after a very short unhappy marriage. Since his childhood, the young man had lived in Rome, the birthplace of his mother. Not too far from his home, he was trained for the clerical field.

Through the efforts of an influential uncle on his mother's side of the family, a man who as high ranking prelate and favourite of the Holy Father had attained almost everything he had desired. However, against all rules and regulations, already as a child he was accepted as a candidate for the order the Maltese Cross. He was now in the process of assuming this responsibility and taking his vows.

The young man's situation was regrettable, since instead of receiving his vocation in this order, which would have been commendable, he was unfortunately in love. Perilously in love! At least he believed this was so. The queen of his heart was a beautiful young lady raised for luxury but absolutely penniless. Her parents had high hopes for their lovely daughter and a pleasant life in a hut was not what they had in mind for her. Lovers should never consider this if they have not been acquainted with this way of live from childhood. But that is another story.

It was quite natural that the young man would rather marry than become a serving brother of the order. Night and day his lovesick lamentations were uttered to his brother. How did his older brother react? He does not employ logic and reason, but allows himself to relent because of his brother's sugar-coated account. Deluded, he does not even examine whether this love is genuine and proper. Instead, he prefers to play a magnanimous role and transfers all his rights and privileges as first-born to his younger brother, so that he may secure this young lady. In consequence, he accepts his position regarding the order, and the uncle in Rome is able to assist him in a thousand ways. Of course this uncle had a thousand reasons why it would be advantageous to help the son of his sister to appropriate these valuable assets. The world would call this arrangement generous and fair. I would call it not only mad but also extremely unfair to all those poor individuals who were naturally dependent upon the older brother to alleviate their own unfortunate circumstances. In his disastrous response, this older brother has left them at the mercy of a love-sick young man, whose monastic education has made him incapable of caring for poor people and who will likely concern himself just as little about real need, as his ancestors did in the last hundred years.

You decide now, Miss, if my views are correct," Lothario bowed as he sat down across from me. "By the way, I have not fabricated this story; a few months ago I witnessed the ceremonial transfer of property. Perhaps some of the guests know our magnanimous hero? His name is Bernhard von Leuen and as far as I know, he spent some time here as well. To top it off, after I left him, he headed for Venice to arrange for passage to Valletta[37] and has probably arrived by now. He was willing to remain several years at headquarters there."

Almost everyone there had known Bernhard von Leuen and many reacted so vehemently that the issue concerning the source of the story was overlooked.

How grateful I was that after this scene I finally found myself alone with my sorrow. Everything I had worked for so diligently since Bernhard had left me, that fragile artificial house of cards where I had sought peace was now destroyed with a single blow. I felt as though pain was consuming me completely now, with all its annihilating consequences. Again, I was unhappier than I had ever been before. Clearly I recognized that any hope of reconciliation or possible atonement for the wrong I had done, or any reunion was lost forever. I shuddered as if I had committed a crime. I was the one, after all, who had prompted this disastrous journey, where he had met his brother.

The distress over me had destroyed the beautiful clarity of his mind and had led him to that impulsive step which was possibly totally unnecessary for the well-being of his brother and had now banned him from his fatherland, reshaped his whole future, robbed him of his property and lead him astray without hope of peace or happiness.

Oh, don't let me speak further about this . . . don't let the ghost of that painful time torture me again. Don't ask me to count the endless days, weeks, years that followed one another . . . without comforting news from him.

The time passed and for my father's sake I tried very hard to appear peaceful and happy. The dignified elderly man edged closer and closer to death as my beautiful sister blossomed and flourished. With an expression of deep concern he often gazed upon this lovely creature who embraced him in youthful exuberance while he turned to me with a pleading look. It hurt me deeply but I withdrew from those imploring eyes. For how would it have been possible for me to choose from among these, for the most part very respectable men, while the memory of Bernhard enveloped my soul; my worrying over him and my regrets about a past that I could not let go!

Though he read my heart, my dear father spared my feelings by never mentioning a word about this subject and did not permit himself to reveal the tiniest intimation of his desire to have me adequately provided for through marriage to a respectable young man, thereby also securing the future of my sister. He never said anything about this but I knew what was going on in his mind and my torment was heightened because I was unable to arrange that which he so passionately sought for his children.

With the unexpected though understandable attitude of your father, Victorine, towards my sister who was barely fifteen years old at the time, all our worries concerning the beloved girl came to a happy end.

Kleeborn was the only son of one of the most respected merchants in the city and he had always been a most faithful and trusted friend of my father. Just then, he had completed the so-called grand tour of most of Europe, which for his class was at that time considered to be essential for the completion of a young man's education. He was now on his way home to find a wife and settle down domestically in the town where he was born.

Like everyone who met her, Kleeborn was captivated by my very pretty sister and her simple cheerful manner. Perhaps seeing her helped him all the more in his selection, since his acquaintance with foreign women was by contrast of a variety that caused him to value a woman like my sister all the more.

Karoline's heart was free and ready to return love, but she was too young to comprehend the significance and scope of this step and so she willingly gave her consent, knowing the happiness it would bring her father.

Both her father and the older Kleeborn believed that the bond between them would be even stronger through the marriage of their children, precluding any possibility of discussions or preconceptions relating to birth or property. Trusting in a happy future, these two directed the betrothed pair swiftly to the altar.

Looking like a blessed saint, my father's eyes shone with unusual brightness during the solemn occasion. Too soon he would actually be counted among them, disappearing to a land where worries dissolve and tears cease to exist! Three days later, we cried over his coffin. With gentle kindness the mild Genius of Death had turned the torch around and softly delivered our dear father to his final peaceful slumber.

I hurried from my father's grave back to the solitude of study that I had learned to love. There, the weak light radiating from my precious friend was not yet entirely extinguished. The flame fought and flickered but continued to burn dimly. I did not want to intrude with my sorrow and cast a shadow over the shining lucky star of the newly wedded pair's blossoming love. Furthermore, I desperately needed rest and quiet.

I was not sick in the strictest sense of the word but the pain I felt over my father and my unexpressed exhaustion were betrayed in an ever increasing depletion of my physical strength and it was so obvious that even our doctor thought my condition serious enough that he recommended a simpler way of life in the country.

I found a kind of peace in my quiet apartment, and solace with my new friendships. But the pain that would not allow me to escape lived in my heart and gnawed furtively at my life.

Early one morning, a few weeks after my arrival, I sat by myself lost in sad reflections. Suddenly, I was startled out of my reverie by Rebecke, my former guardian who flung the door open with an unaccustomed urgency. This faithful soul had taken care of both me and my sister since birth, and was like a mother to us. So, despite her advanced age, it was out of the question that she would permit me to withstand my seclusion unaccompanied. She maintained that I needed to be cared for and she understood this better than anyone else.

"*Fräulein Annettchen*[38]," she cried quite out of breath. She had always called me *Annettchen* since childhood. "*Fräulein Annettchen*, imagine with whom I have just been speaking! He was walking in the gardens. Herr von Leuen! He recognized me immediately and was beaming with happiness. And he asked me a lot of questions about your situation. I showed him your windows and he seemed to find the wild vines with the pretty red leaves very attractive. In any case he looked at them for some time and admired them."

Dear Lord! How can I describe this feeling that came over me when I received this message? It was like awakening from a ghostly slumber. I hugged the dear old woman and laughed and cried with delirious happiness. I kneeled and thanked God out loud that Bernard still remembered me. Then a deadly anxiety overcame me once more and I cautioned dear Rebecke again to consider whether she had not been mistaken about this person. I made her describe in detail what he looked like; I asked a hundred times if he truly would come. Still, I could not believe that he was really here because of me and that I would see him again.

Rebecke patiently repeated what she had already told me a thousand times. Since then, I have never let this faithful friend leave my side. Years later, with childlike gratitude, I took care of her, until weary of life, she passed away in my arms. I always remembered that it was Rebecke who first told me that Bernhard von Leuen had returned.

After a few hours he actually came. I really did see him again. Dear children, I am very old and many many years have passed since that moment. But when I think about him, I feel as though the grey hair on my forehead is once more a shimmering cascade of bright curls. It is as if a radiant beam of light from above is giving me back my youth. He was very happy to see me again and that I was so well, for the delight of this blessed moment gave my otherwise gaunt appearance a look of health and coloured my pale cheeks with a rosy hue.

Bernhard said that he had heard in my native city that I was probably suffering from an incurable illness and he confessed that he was so worried about me that his only reason for coming was to see me, even if he would see me only at a distance. He told me this succinctly, in the fewest possible words, but his eyes betrayed his feelings. Neither of us said much during this first meeting; we were not able to speak for we were so happy. It was as though the oppressive past had never existed.

The next morning he came again. However, new doubts seemed to have entered his mind. He stood before me despondent and withdrawn. I calmly endured this change in his behaviour because I knew that I deserved it. Recklessly, I had played with his confidence.

But true to myself, I did not think about this and did not want anything other than to be open and sincere, to show myself as I was, without artifice, without contrivance, as far as I was able to without compromising the dignity of my womanhood. I did not want to risk losing his respect again in any way.

On the third day he came to say goodbye. I led him to the provost. Exhausted from an unusual bout of pain, she had not been able to see him earlier and still felt rather weak. Only through my urgent appeals had she agreed to receive my friend. It meant so much to me that if he would now depart from me forever, I would at least have the consolation of saying his name and hearing his voice, even if rife with indifference. I was well aware that all who knew him, would never refer to him as completely indifferent.

An unexpected matter which the provost was not able to take care of because of her illness was assigned to me and compelled me to leave her room just as I was ushering Bernhard into the room.

I was detained for almost an hour and when I returned, contrary to my expectations, he was still with my friend but it seemed to me that his mood had noticeably changed. There was a hastiness in his movements that was quite foreign to his nature as well as a fire in his eyes and the expression of anguish that I knew so well.

All this seemed to indicate that something unusual had happened to him since I left the room.

The provost lay exhausted and pale in her bed but like a saint she smiled at me and indicated I was to approach. In low voice, she instructed me to continue the discussion with Herr von Leuen and to excuse her illness.

After I indicated that we should leave, Bernhard followed me with a very conspicuous urgency. His arm trembled as he led me down the stairs. He was obviously in emotional turmoil, although I was not able to determine the nature of it.

I had hardly returned alone to room, when the storm inside me, restrained only with great difficulty, finally broke free.

"Anna, dear long lost and found again Anna," he cried as he looked at me, as if I were a sorely missed precious gem, examining it with rough hands and eyes that shone with pure delight.

"Yes, it's you," he continued in a voice brimming with emotion. "And you are still the same. Precious and pure as an angel sent from Heaven. Unaware of what she was doing, your friend has torn away the veil that has hidden you from me for such a long time. She spoke of you of the gratitude and deep affection that she so rightly feels for you. Anna, I know now all about the unselfish life you have lived from the moment I heartlessly fled from you. I can almost say that I know how you have spent each quarter-hour of that long, long time. What I had suspected the first time I saw you again and I was so blind that I resisted for a long time, has been made very clear to me in this hour . . . and I am both the happiest and most unhappy man on earth!"

Dear children, what else can I tell you about the conversation of these two . . . lost in pain and ecstasy? Bernhard confessed how he had arrived at his castle deeply hurt, without a plan, incapable even of devising a plan. There, grappling with wild despair, he encountered his brother. Everything Lothario had shown as objectionable and repulsive I saw now moderated through a thousand circumstances . . . in the lovely light of the most noble sacrifice, he wanted to provide a loving couple with the happiness from which he appeared to be hopelessly and forever excluded. He could not wait any longer in Malta, he told me.

"I was overwhelmed with an uncontrollable yearning; something like the homesickness of the Swiss. I had to leave again . . . I could not endure a life any longer where I did not know what was happening to you. I took a holiday and returned to Germany so I could verify that you were alive, and that you were happy. At least those were my intentions. But when I was in your vicinity again, I realized this was not enough. I had to see you again. And then I found you! And you were exactly the way you appeared in my happiest dreams!"

Unfortunately the rapture of the present moment was nothing but a fleeting heavenly dream that too soon gave way to a harsh reality. For as soon as the first happy euphoria passed away, I had a premonition that we had only found each other to lose each other again. We would be left only with the solid faith that we meant something to each other and would remain so forever. Love expanded my heart and raised my spirits. I confessed everything and apologized for every wrong I had committed. I revealed the depth of my soul before his loving eyes. He too unmasked his soul to me and I enjoyed the bliss of forgiving as he did.

When we were more composed we considered our present situation and future as far as we were able to . . . to see if there were a solution for us . . . some hope of retrieving the happiness that we had forfeited. Alas! Although it hurt both of us, we had to admit that each in our own way had resigned ourselves forever to the impossibility of a closer tie between us.

Bernhard was Catholic. Although he had never made a secret of this, I was not aware of this earlier. For in my absolute indifference regarding anything religious, I had never thought it worth my while to explore this further. In accepting the Maltese Cross, he had dedicated himself to a life of celibacy. Certainly the Pope could release him from his vows and it probably would not have been difficult to obtain this favour, but then Bernhard would lose the associated income and all he had was a small annuity that he had safeguarded for himself. His brother, to whom he had transferred everything that he once owned, was not capable of assisting him under any circumstances. His lavish lifestyle and equally extravagant wife who was accustomed to living in splendour, led Bernhard's brother into a life of debt and financial embarrassment. Consequently, he had encumbered the income from his already diminished assets for years to come.

As a protestant canoness, I was not hindered by vows, but my father had not left me very much money either, although I did have the income from a little capital in conjunction with my stipend which was adequate for my needs.

Bernhard shuddered at the thought of dragging me, his beloved, down into a deep abyss of misery and deprivation, and felt that he had no other choice but renunciation. My dear friend was close to despair about this, because he blamed our sad fate on a combative rashness which was entirely foreign to his character and a reaction against the overwhelming painful assault on his emotions at that time. And the realization that his brother had not found happiness he had hoped for at the side of a wife so dearly acquired completely robbed Bernhard of any possible consolation.

And though I had known a far harsher pain and was now in tears, I was happy. I tried to convey to Bernhard this wistful calm, a feeling that has never left me entirely since that unforgettable hour. But unfortunately my urging and appeals were no match against his deep-rooted sorrow.

"Bernhard," I said to him. "Believe me, from now on, I will wear this punishment of my past recklessness not only with resignation, but with tranquil happiness. From now on, my life will be faithfully and completely dedicated to you, no matter what fate may have in store for us. And even though we may never meet again after today; and if after the painful separation that will soon be upon us I never again see the beloved figure of my friend again, I will remain faithful to you . . . only to you. Because we are one . . . forever . . . and the vow that binds you binds me as well."

Bernhard shuddered fiercely in response to my resolution. Almost kneeling, he implored me to stop.

"You don't understand what kind of a sacrifice you are making with your noble gesture. Your life is just beginning to bloom, and you will only be young once. Don't squander both on an unfortunate soul who must be punished because he did not want to believe in you . . . someone who forged his own chains in blind delusion and now cannot break them. Dear Anna, imagine that I have died today . . . wear my memory in your pure and faithful mind as you would for someone you once loved who has passed away. Remember me with peaceful serenity when you are happy . . . I cannot ask for more. But promise me at least that you will not dismiss happiness on my account, should it approach you in a form worthy of you . . . and this will certainly happen and soon.

For me, the world and happiness no longer exist . . . I am only the tombstone of what I once was."

His passionate pleas and the tears that clouded his beautiful eyes moved me deeply, not because his reasoning shattered my intentions, but simply because his pleas were addressed to me. I cried with him, but I stood firm. And so we parted that same evening, for a long, long time, because Bernhard's return to Malta could not be altered.

Again, I remained alone, but how differently everything turned out. Bernhard's letters were few and far between because of the great distance, but they became the most essential element of my life. My whole existence was centred around receiving his letters and the pleasure of answering them. Every anniversary date of our separation bound us closer to one another, weaving our lives together in the most beautiful way through this written communication of all our inner and external experiences. If ever two people deserved to be called one, we did.

Occasionally, I had to separate myself for a few months from the solitude that had become so dear to me in order to visit my sister who lived in the hustle and bustle of the world. But as soon as I was able to, without offending my sister, I would return to my solitude, full of longing.

On my way home again, surveying the old tower of my cloistral apartment from a distance, my heart would pound with unbridled joy. It was almost as if I was certain to find Bernhard there again; I lived for him and knew no other happiness except for my preoccupation with him, a preoccupation to which I could happily devote myself without interruptions.

The world soon forgot me, just as it eventually forgets everything and so I was able to live a quiet, solemn life for a number of years.

I would even venture to say a happy life, known by few and envied by none.

Meanwhile, the world struggled with dangerous conflicts. The French Revolution had begun and everything, *everything* including the realm of ideas as well as the world in actuality experienced a terrible and violent transformation. Only a few were able to escape this turmoil completely.

Even my friend could not endure this watching from a distance; he could not continue to live peacefully amid the wild tumult in the rest of Europe. That seemed like passivity to him and he tried everything to extricate himself, at least for a while.

He came back to his own country. Notably, he hurried to locate me again in my solitude and for a second time we celebrated an enchanting though simultaneously more melancholy reunion. Then he set forth again, out into the turbulent world to observe developments close at hand. Noble youth everywhere had been blinded by the deceptive glimmer of true freedom and prodigious civic pride that had been propagated at the beginning of the Revolution. From a distance, Bernhard too was stirred by the general frenzy, but as he approached, the illusion faded fairly quickly. Nature had given him astute powers of perception.

The allied powers now rose and joined forces against this multi-headed Hydra[39] of most savage anarchy; to suffocate it right from the start. Bernhard also joined their army and shared with his noble comrades the evil of that dark and perilous time.

Deeply troubled after a bitter campaign, he hurried back to me. He sought and found comfort and reassurance with me, the only person in the world to whom he still felt connected. By the grace of a great monarch with whom he had fortunately become acquainted during that extraordinary war, he received an offer, so he left again to associate himself with a wider sphere of activity.

His Maltese obligations, possibly his vows as well were as good as extinguished or at least suspended because Malta through cowardice and shameful treachery also fell into the hands of familiar world robbers. Completely free from that quarter, Bernhard now began to lead a very purposeful and prodigious life, which he fortunately knew how to advance very well through his multiple connections with powerful and distinguished contemporaries. In actual fact, his intelligence, his scientific education, his life experience, and his disarming personality paved the way for him everywhere he went.

Meanwhile, my surroundings had undergone a significant change as well. Finally, after a long struggle, the noble pure spirit of my friend was released from painful earthly bonds and yielded to eternity. For years now, due to the restrictions of her illness, I had managed under her supervision, all duties for which she had been responsible in her capacity as Provost of the foundation.

After her death, against my expectations and without a word from me, I was chosen as her successor which meant that I was now responsible for the management of numerous estates belonging to the foundation. This opened the door to a wide range of possibilities where I could exercise my intellectual strengths and thousand-fold opportunities to do something useful and beneficial.

In the meantime, my friend was engaged as foreign envoy to his monarch, alternating between many and some rather distant courts, and the brilliant splendour that surrounded him in his current field of activity often concealed him from me. Yet even far away, he was still mine and I remained the sole *confidante* of his plans, his impressions, his actions; in fact, every thought in his soul. Sometimes with the advice I was able to offer him, I managed to be useful in other ways.

With this regular and sometimes rather active participation with matters usually outside a woman's sphere, I eventually developed surprising intellectual abilities; a completely different kind of education as was customary in my *milieu*. My inner strength grew, as well as my power over individuals with whom I came into contact. I was very busy and this had a beneficial effect on my health. Over the course of time, I managed to achieve a lot of good. I might add that I was able to bring out the best in many who trusted me and were attracted to my way of life. But my friend protected me from smugness; I was and always remained the echo of his beliefs and of his life.

After a few years Bernhard returned from abroad in order to be near to the monarch whom he served; a rather influential position. We saw each other again, and we separated again and met frequently in the course of our lives but always rediscovered our familiar abiding loyalty, just as we had left each other. Occasionally, I would spend several months in Bernard's pleasant companionship, when business did not permit him to call on me to break my solitude at the usual time.

Bernhard was affluent again now and it was in his power to dissolve his vows. He would have been able to offer me an alliance for the rest of our lives and he would have gladly made public to the world that no matter what fate had in store for him, his life was dedicated only to me. But we two had grown old in the meantime and we did not have the courage to make a quick decision. We were also inhibited by a strange shyness and neither of us could account for this in a clear explanation. This deterred us from altering our happy long-standing relationship in any way. One year after another passed by and in the meantime, we probably would have admitted that each new separation awakened a desire to spend the rest of our days in undisturbed togetherness.

Then death came between us. Bernhard passed away in distant Switzerland, where his master's business had summoned him. My deep anguish drew me to his grave where I surrendered my tears; the first release for the numb bitterness I felt in my breast.

When I surveyed the wonders of nature in that beautiful country, the iron band clenching my heart seemed to dissolve and in the hills of Switzerland I thought I would cry out my life forever for my beloved lost to me for all eternity. My burdened heart was comforted, my eyes lifted once again with devout hope and resignation to the sovereign above the eternal mountains who reveals himself more closely to mortals through the magnitude of nature. I stayed in Switzerland long enough so that I would be at his grave on the anniversary of his death. It has been eight years now . . . as of today."

CHAPTER 16

Vite! Vite, mes enfants, hurry to the window! *Ciel de Dieu, quel train*! Mamsell Virnot was shouting with excitement as she thrust her head through the partially opened living room door. But almost immediately she withdrew and hurried away. Babet and Agathe were sitting all alone at the fireplace, diligently occupied with their sewing.

Agathe, as she rose in her hasty careless manner, upset the large embroidery hoop, becoming entangled in the threads of the spools of silk that were rolling across the floor and impetuously tore everything apart as she hurried to open the window. The blaring sound of many competing postilions coming closer and closer was an irresistible attraction for her. Babet joined her and both girls stretched out their necks in eager curiosity and anticipation towards the approaching troupe of travellers.

"Close the window!" thundered Herr Kleeborn, who had just entered the room.

"Are you out of your mind, in this cold? Do you want to heat the road? And all your paraphernalia all over the floor! This is a fine state of affairs!"

"Oh, dear uncle," cried Babet without turning her head towards him. "Just close the door quickly so we don't get a horrible draft."

"And don't scold," added Agathe as she winked at him with a smile. "You should come and look with us instead . . . the cavalry are riding through!"

"Cavalry, why not?" said Babet shrugging her shoulders with disdain. "They will lodge in the *Hotel d'Angleterre*. They seem to be very distinguished!"

His curiosity roused by the chattering of the girls the uncle approached to peer over their heads. Attracted by the increasing noise on the street, the aunt, Victorine and Angelika had come into the room right behind the uncle and were now gathering in front of the second window.

Diagonally across from the Kleeborn home, they were able to see the entire *Hotel d'Angleterre* bustling with activity. Surrounded by his group of waiters in third position from the front door and ready to make the deepest bows, stood the normally very distinguished-looking master of the house. The entire staff looked with eager expectation towards the side of the street from where the sound of the post horn came near ever louder and merrier.

To the amusement of the gathering of young people, a stunning rider in colourful attire had just descended from his horse and with the greatest composure he lead the steaming animal up and down the narrow street. As the horse cooled off, the servants were prodigiously occupied with a heavy-laden baggage wagon, carrying the curiously shaped suitcases and coat trunks to the depot. It appeared that the baggage wagon belonged to a very elegant carriage drawn by four post horses which was only able to approach the hotel as the baggage wagon moved aside.

Two stylishly dressed young men sat in the carriage; a servant sat on an appropriate and comfortably furnished seat and a magnificent hunter and a young black boy in brilliant colours were mounted on the horse in front.

"There they are," whispered the girls as they nudged each other without looking, so captivated were they by the strangers who were being assisted with fawning servility out of the carriage by the hotel-keeper.

"*Ce sont des Mylords anglais*," old Virnot cried out from below to the window above. Out of curiosity, she too had been lured to the front door.

"On the contrary! A travelling young Prince or a count with his steward," stated Herr Kleeborn with great resolution as he was about to chase the girls away from the window and close it. But he refrained from doing so, because to his astonishment he noticed that the strangers who had just stepped out of the carriage were not being directed to the house. Instead, they remained standing in front of the house with the hotel-keeper, waiter and servants, as if they were still waiting for someone. At the same time, the heads of several horses and their riders loomed at a distance, above the large crowd of spectators, and as often happens in large and smaller cities, they stopped on the street.

"Listen, the one on the right is still coming, I think," whispered Babet to Agathe. "Probably a king, and those are only his ministers."

"Oh, let me see!" answered Agathe. "Look at the horses! They're wearing coats and proper hats with ears and have red trimming on their noses."

"Of course they might be performers after all," cheered the young girl and clapped her hands with joy. "That would be magnificent! We haven't seen any in a long while."

"Three horses covered from top to bottom in grey cloaks with red trimming were now being led by two mounted grooms and a striking man dressed in a modern dark coat rode alongside.

"You see, I was right!" exulted Agathe. "That is the master of the troupe and the women are probably sitting there in the last carriage. Dear Uncle, it is true, are they really performers?" She turned to her uncle with a smile.

"It almost looks that way to me as well," answered Kleeborn. "Most likely Tourniaire. They say that the man is quite wealthy. But I am surprised that he is stopping here at the first hotel of the city with all those people and horses. It will cost him a lot of money."

"So? Who is correct now?" cried Babet and leaned as far as possible towards the window. Where do you see ladies? The king or prince is just arriving now in that beautiful large carriage."

"No, that is a woman in a man's clothing," declared Agathe. "Performers always travel that way. You can see that she has a dog with her and a monkey. Certainly they will perform their artistry with fireworks, just as I read in the newspaper. I don't see the tame deer yet. They will likely come after with all the rest of the ensemble. Oh, dear, beloved favourite uncle . . . we *must* go and see their performance on the first day! How lucky for us! We will see this musical parade swirl by twice each day . . . when they depart and when they return."

A very elegant folded-back Landau carriage drawn by six horses approached very slowly because of the rather narrow street filled with pedestrians. It was empty except for a young man who sat in a corner or rather stretched out comfortably in a most careless position, as if he was at home on his own sofa. A luxurious fur coat of an extraordinary design covered him up to his ears and he wore green goggles that gave his pale though not unpleasant face a frightful ghost-like appearance. He was so absorbed in reading a newspaper that he did not look away even for an instant. Beside him sat a fine large dog with tiger stripes. He had planted his front paws on the shoulders of his master and was diligently and dutifully studying the newspaper, as if he understood the contents. A delightful little house decorated with golden latticework was positioned on the back seat of the carriage. On the roof of this little house, sat a chained long-tailed monkey who bared his teeth with a loud screech and threw the remains of his *en-route* meal on the heads of the local boys surrounding the carriage. This did not seem to bother his master in the least and he continued to read his newspaper undisturbed all the way to the *Hotel d'Angleterre.*

Slowly, as if awakening from a pleasant snooze, the traveller stepped out of the carriage, whistled for his dog who followed at his heels, and indicated to the black boy that he was to carry the monkey. With proud bearing, he entered the hotel without acknowledging the hotel-keeper or his compliments. All followed him respectfully; the hotel-keeper, the servants, the waiters and finally the two strangers who had arrived just shortly before. The horses were led away, the spectators dispersed and Kleeborn carefully closed the window. And the pageant was over for the time being.

"See how you have embarrassed yourself again," Babet reproached Agathe. "You with your horsemen! That's what happens when you always think that you know everything better than other people."

"But we aren't really certain that they are not performers," replied Agathe rather sheepishly. "They just might be horsemen, though very refined, perhaps they have just come from London."

"Right across the Mediterranean Sea on horseback?" mocked Babet with a sarcastic smile.

"For God's sake, please be quiet," interrupted Herr Kleeborn. "Your candidate would be amused by your knowledge of geography, if he could hear you now. At least this much is clear. They are definitely not performers. Maybe one of the English princes? But they are all much older. I know . . . I will simply send Johann over."

The servant was immediately sent on *reconnaissance* and did not return until Kleeborn and his family had been gathered quite some time at the lavishly set breakfast table. In large commercial centres the midday meal was delayed to a time which in other regions already belonged to the afternoon.

Impatiently they looked for their envoy and the good uncle was no less plagued by curiosity as were his nieces, but the news that Johann brought back did not satisfy their curiosity. A genteel and refined group they were. This is what the house-master had said. But other than that, he knew nothing, other than that the entire *bel-étage*[40] of his house was to be confiscated for several weeks and that on account of them the existing occupants had to be moved to other rooms which was naturally not possible without great awkwardness and aggravation.

"And furthermore," continued Johann. "Furthermore, everything was topsy-turvy at the hotel. The cook, and the waiters and chambermaid continually bumping into one another trying to keep our guests and their attendants happy, which was not easy because they made a thousand and one demands all at once and each wanted something different."

Meanwhile, Agathe and Babet drew near to the window again to watch the monkey opposite them also sitting on the window ledge and the crowd that had gathered again in front of the house to observe the amusing antics of the comical little animal.

"Listen," whispered Agathe sitting half on her knees and half on an upside down footstool trying to put her embroidery frame back into order. "Listen, Babet! Maybe it is the King of Heidi or whatever his name is, the one who is supposed to marry the Saxon *Mamsel* that everyone is talking about and perhaps he is coming now to fetch his bride. If only Count *Limonade* or *Schokolade* were with him!"

"Silly child, they are already dead and gone," lectured Babet.

"Oh how should I know if all those people are living or dead," answered Agathe indignantly and repositioned one of the tapestry spools that had taken flight.

"This much we know for sure," pondered Babet with great deliberation, after Agathe sat beside her again. "We do know that the stranger has a reliable address. So our uncle should give a ball in his honour. That is the least that one could do for such a noteworthy person."

"Well, thank goodness!" cried Agathe and clapped her little hands. "Thank goodness, then we will have a little life in this house again."

"Yes, but I will tell you one thing. I refuse to wear that pink *crepon*[41]. That tall Schmidt girl has a dress exactly like mine. My gold tulle[42] must be ready in time and you must help me."

"If he were a prince . . . a real prince," continued Agathe a little dubiously. "I have never really seen a prince close up in my life. And if only he would dance with me!"

"Of course he will dance with us. We are the ladies of the house," Babet corrected. "It's only a shame that my Theodor won't be there. He would probably be out of his mind with jealousy if he had to watch the prince paying court to me.

"I would be scared to death if he were to dance with me," cried Agathe. "He probably only dances the *Française*. If only *Monsieur* Michaud were here, so that we could practice the *Pas* a little."

"If he is English, he probably only dances *Ekossais*[43] and very likely does not know how to waltz, unfortunately," added Babet.

"*Pas de Zéphyr*," called out Agathe, as she raised her skirt and tried out different dance steps in front of the large mirror.

"*Tour de bras, en avant! Tournez! Rigadon*," joined in Babet. "*Allons, tour de poule.*"

"*Tour de* Goose would suit you two better," interjected Herr Kleeborn with a laugh as he watched the two girls amiably. At this particular moment they really were quite adorable.

"Dear Lord, Uncle! The stranger is coming to our house!" cried Agathe who had just looked out the window.

"He is not the right one," pointed out the Babet excitedly.

"How do you know, for sure?" asked Agathe. "Dear, kind, favourite Uncle," she coaxed in her most charming manner. "Please, please do me a little favour and let him come in. I would so much like to see him close up.

Mr. Wilkinson from London. That is how the stranger introduced himself. As he walked in to the room, everyone recognized him as one of the two men who had arrived in the first carriage. He was a handsome young man dressed in the latest English fashion. As he walked through the door, he gracefully ran the fingers of his left hand through his resplendent hair while he removed his hat with his right hand, very courteously greeting first the ladies then the man of the house with a graceful nod of the head. He had a foreign accent but spoke German fluently.

"Sir Charles Wissmann has respectfully recommended that I present myself to the ladies and Master Kleeborn."

"Wissmann," responded Kleeborn with delight and heartily shook the stranger's hand. "Wissmann! Well, my dear Mr Wilkinson, you are most welcome to our home. But why didn't he come directly to me? I had invited him and his rooms are available. Babet, go child and let *Mamsell* Virnot know that she should open and heat up the rooms."

Babet poked Agathe with her elbow indicating that *she* should go, but neither girl made a move, neither wanted to desert the focus of their collective attention.

"Oh, please don't trouble the *Fräulein*" requested Wilkinson. "Sir Charles would not want to disturb the family and since we need a fair amount of space . . ."

"I have enough room," replied Kleeborn. "You are probably the travelling companion of the young Wissmann. I assure you that I have enough room for you as well and you are just as welcome in my home, my dear Mr. Wilkinson. Four rooms are available . . . that should meet the needs of the two young gentlemen. Well then, the young man who sat beside you . . . that is, you should know that we saw you disembark in front of the hotel. The young man then, is he the son of my old friend? Well, well, who would have known? Now then, what about you? Are you also a man of business? You are right, that is the best profession in the world."

"Pardon, me," answered the stranger in a measured tone of voice. "Pardon me, sir. I have the pleasure of being associated with Sir Charles in the capacity of secretary. The young man who sat beside me in the carriage serves him as *homme de chambre*. Actually he should have been on the horse. But as you know, we don't take such formalities so seriously when we travel and in any case Marcellin is so devoted to his master that for that reason alone much is overlooked."

"So . . ." drawled Kleeborn with half a whistle, half a sigh. He paused a moment then added with a somewhat dejected look, "so, is Wissmann not there then? Maybe not coming today?"

"Pardon me," replied Wilkinson. "You mentioned before that you saw us disembark at the front of the hotel. Well, Sir Charles' Landau[44] was right behind me."

"Oh? I see. Hm . . . " replied Kleeborn with mounting astonishment and decreasing optimism. "and the horses?"

"Good Heavens! They are beautiful animals!" Wilkinson added. "As you will have no doubt noticed. Especially the light brown horse . . . Sir Charles' favourite. No one can command that spirited animal other than his master and the groom. The horse is a direct descendent from the Duke of Bedford's famous Hector. Orion was his father; a five-time winner at Newmarket. His mother was Lord Ashford's Molly and at the last race in Epsom . . ."

"Look here!" Kleeborn interrupted the suddenly eloquent secretary's long-winded recital of horse pedigrees and heroic deeds with respect to his future son-in-law. "Yes, yes, but what about Herr Wissmann?"

"Sir Charles," replied Wilkinson. "Sir Charles has requested that I announce his happy arrival to you and your family. A personal note from him would have been better and more appropriate. However, Domingo lost the key to his master's briefcase and was obliged through me to ask that you kindly excuse this appreciable contravention of etiquette. Certainly only an exigency would have necessitated this request, in this case the writing materials offered by the house master were completely unsatisfactory."

"This surprises me, since that man is usually very orderly." said Kleeborn.

"Completely unsatisfactory, I assure you," repeated Wilkinson. "Incidentally, Sir Charles would like to request your permission to visit you and the ladies this evening. He merely needs to change his travelling clothes and rest a while from his journey. We are accustomed to travel quickly but the roads in this region are in rather poor condition."

Brimming with politeness and decorum, the secretary finally left the room and Kleeborn had time to recover a little from the astonishment of all he had witnessed. His face was like a day in April; now bright with the joy of sunshine, and in the next moment the looming darkness of angry storm clouds hovered over him.

Whistling quietly, he paced from one corner of the room to another, as was his habit whenever his composure was upset and everyone remaining in the room appeared to be equally anxious. Babet and Agathe were transfixed as images of the prince, the secretary, Sir Charles, and the horsemen twirled tumultuously through their minds. Angelika, who had participated little in the preceding events now quietly crept away to Victorine. Leaning over the back of her chair, she observed her beloved friend with a look that simultaneously expressed deep affection and concern.

Although Victorine appeared conspicuously more pale than usual, her eyes sparkled and she held her head high as she sat proudly beside her aunt. She looked as if she were courageously looking forward to battle.

Anna's fine mouth revealed an almost imperceptible mocking smile as her keen eyes observed every movement of Victorine's father. A few more times he paced back and forth in the room with large strides and then suddenly stopped in front of Victorine as if he wanted to say something. But just as suddenly he turned around and started to pace once more. There was a deathly silence in the room which no one dared to disturb.

"Hm," Kleeborn said finally partly to himself partly to the others. "Hm, yes . . . he does require a secretary as Dutch consul in London. Although for travelling I would think . . . well, times have changed a great deal since I was a young man. Certainly I did not travel as much, but as the saying goes, other times, other customs. And with the backing this young man has . . . well . . . hm."

A new pause and another promenade ensued, then the old man stopped in front of his daughter.

"Victorine," he began. "You have heard who has arrived, or I should say whom we are awaiting. That's why I thought, my child, that you should use this time before we sit down at the table to make yourself pretty."

"Dear Uncle! The same applies to us," interrupted Babett with her bright little voice.

"Are you still here too?" he snapped. "You may do as you like. Who will pay attention to you?"

Quiet as a mouse she crept away along the carpet towards the door and winked at Agathe. Both girls disappeared. Likewise, Angelika followed them pursuant to a wink from Anna.

"My dear sister," Kleeborn began as he sat down beside the aunt and reached for her hand. "Dear sister, you are a very wise woman. I know this and I know you will be fair and reasonable. This young man whom we saw arriving across the street about an hour ago, certainly with eye-catching pageantry is, as I now know, the son of one of the most prominent families in Amsterdam, one whose wealth allows for privileges and luxury excluded to others. In some respects I would even praise him for purposely choosing to parade his brilliance right here. What I am referring to will not escape your famous insight, but back to my point. Ten years ago, when the whole world had abandoned me . . . friends and relatives . . . yes, dear sister, even relatives upon whom I should have been able to depend . . . my blood boils when I think about this. You of course are innocent, there was nothing you could have done. Enough of this! This young man's father saved more than my life. Even you, Victorine, even you owe him something. That's it! It's all over, thank God and our honour survived intact. One thing is certain, though. We would not be where we are today without my old friend from Amsterdam. And I would have been long . . . well, as I said it's all past history. But I will repay the son for all the help given to me by the father. That's stating it about as clearly as is possible for an honest man. And no one should contradict me when I say that it is the duty of my only child to help me fulfill my obligation. So go now, Victorine! Go and change your clothes."

"I will do this if you absolutely demand it," replied Victorine with deep emotion, as her father's command seemed to require. "I will do as you ask, but permit me to say that I am convinced that I can properly receive all company just as I am dressed at this moment. And even though I am prepared to receive the son of your friend, who means so much to you with the courtesy required of me as your daughter, I do not understand why I should make an exception on this point."

"An exception!" exclaimed Kleeman with irritation.

"Yes, father, an exception," repeated Victorine in a demure but firm manner. "I simply ask you not to forget the past, just as I will never forget my obligation to you. My word should not be less valid than yours. I am your daughter and I will prove my respect for your friend's son. As soon as he manoeuvres me into having to explain myself to him I will clarify any doubt about my heart, my situation and my final decision. This is no secret to you father, so I ask you to . . ."

"Victorine!" shouted Kleeborn, his face contorted with rage as he jumped up. The aunt stepped between father and daughter in an effort to calm them.

"You are both the strangest of people!" she cried smiling. "I realize now what you are both talking about. But Victorine, do you think that a young man of the world as he seems to be, would so suddenly appear before you like a *Hochzeitbitter*[45] from the country and make a wedding speech? And you, my dear brother, I am sure that you can see that Victorine is still mending from a frightful struggle with her illness. In any case, sick children are always spoiled a little and this requires our indulgence afterwards.

"Yes, yes, you are quite right, sister," replied Kleeborn who appeared to have simmered down upon hearing her words. "You are right . . . *time* . . . time alone works wonders. Time cures everything. Everything is found in time."

Reciting his favourite and most often repeated words of consolation, the old man left the room and hurried to the stock exchange. Due to the events of the morning, for the first time in his life he had almost forgotten about it. The late mid-day meal in the Kleeborn household had been very quiet and was now long over as evening descended steadily towards nightfall. The long row of windows along the first floor of the *Hotel d'Angleterre* shimmered with an almost blinding light, as if some grand festivity were taking place. Meanwhile, Kleeborn with increasing impatience paced in front of the rooms that had been designated for his guests waiting in vain for his expected visitors.

"Just as I thought," he cried stamping his foot as the clock struck ten. But just at that moment, the door was flung open and Sir Charles entered the room, looking like someone cut out of the latest fashion magazine. Quick as a wink, a beam of delight spread over Kleeborn's face, replacing all trace of his earlier disgruntlement.

They discussed each other's latest developments for half an hour before they realized how much time had gone by. Then Kleeborn took the arm of his young friend and brought him to the livingroom to introduce his family. They had just reached the entry when old Müller stormed up the stairs behind them.

"Herr Kleeborn, a word please!" he cried breathlessly. "A courier has just come; probably the long awaited news from . . ."

"Marvellous!" interjected Kleeborn with delight. "My dear Herr Wissmann," he said after thinking a moment. "Please forgive me; I will be back in ten minutes. Meanwhile, I would like to introduce my daughter." Kleeborn opened the door and without looking nudged the young man into the living room. His mind already on business that awaited him, he hurried away to his office.

Despite his self-assurance and the high opinion he had of himself, Sir Charles felt if perhaps not self-conscious, at least a little embarrassed that he would be pushed towards his intended bride in this most unusual manner. But the young lady whom he encountered alone in the room received him so graciously that every impulse of strangeness disappeared like fog dispersed by the sun.

The way she responded with two quick curtsies to his first greeting, the little dimples below blushing cheeks that looked like peaches in a slightly bashful smiling face, and the gracious pantomime with which she obliged him to sit in the sofa, all this was more than was needed to help a young man of his nature feel comfortable. After his first glance at the beautiful young lady, he flung himself into a corner of the sofa beside her with all the amiable negligence of a genuine English dandy of the finest style. Through his glasses he keenly regarded her, from the tortoiseshell comb that arranged the lustrous light brown braids on her head, to the tip of the tiny pretty feet that were daintily trying to trace the contour of the large roses on the rug. The pearly-white teeth visible through the slightly open youthful lips, the mischievous smiling eyes, the round arms and tiny dimpled hands, the plump and yet petite frame, in short, this composite of roses and snow pleased him exceedingly the more he looked at her.

Finally he ventured to lift the timid eyes of his neighbour in his direction. Of course at first she would lower her eyes almost immediately, but gradually she gained the courage using her naive coquetry, and personal charms in order to present herself to him in the most advantageous light. Instinctively she may have felt that she was successful in her endeavors and in a short time both felt quite happy with themselves and with each other. Although Kleeborn should have properly introduced them, they did not miss him in the least.

Although the topic of conversation at the beginning proceeded at a snail's pace and focused on roads and weather and how tiring a journey in winter can be, neither were bored in the slightest. And when Sir Charles' magnificent horses were mentioned, the conversation took on a livelier gait and quite naturally the topic drifted to the cute monkey, that most interesting travelling partner. Sir Charles related some amusing anecdotes where the main role was played by his Koko. The stories made the young girl laugh and Sir Charles was so delighted by her laughter that he continued with his tales and she laughed all the more heartily.

The conversation was refreshing and stimulating and neither thought it would ever succumb to boredom. Who knows how long Sir Charles would have stayed before he would come to the realization that he should leave. However after half an hour Kleeborn sent his regrets that important business threatened to keep him in his office until the late hours and prevented him from returning. This was clearly a sign that required a response from Sir Charles, reluctant as it might be.

"Actually she, my future bride, is not a beauty, though she is definitely extraordinarily pretty," he murmured contentedly to himself without the slightest clue that he could have been mistaken about this person. He crossed the street to go to his apartment.

As is customary for an Englishman, in the course of the conversation he had always referred to Kleeborn by name and not as the father of the young lady with whom he was speaking. This confusing outcome was not exactly in Babet's plan.

As the reader has probably guessed by now, it was Babet and not Victorine whom Sir Charles had met in the living room. The reason that Babet remained all alone in the living room is because Anna, Agathe and Victorine were tired of waiting so long for the expected guest, so they withdrew for the evening. Babet, on the other hand, was a little vexed at having spent so much effort in preening and primping all for nothing. So without saying a word to anyone, she decided to wait a little longer to see if this stranger whose arrival this morning had aroused their curiosity to the extreme would not come after all. When he actually came into the living room, she soon realized that he had mistaken her for Victorine and the embarrassed silence promptly gave way to something more deliberate when she discovered that the young man found her attractive.

"He didn't ask for my name after all," she thought. "And besides, is it my fault if he likes me better than Victorine? It would be silly of me to immediately refuse him. In the end, I am probably doing Victorine a favour because as far as I can see it seems she has something else on her mind besides this Sir Charles, whom her father has chosen for her.

After Charles left, Babet hurried to her sister, brimming with the conquest she felt that she had made so unexpectedly late that evening. She wanted to share this memorable event but Agathe was almost in the grip of sleep and rather unresponsive.

"Oh, go away," she said finally since Babet would not stop talking. "That's enough about your Englishman. If he isn't a prince or a knight then I don't need to know anything about him and don't be cross with me but I cannot praise you for allowing yourself to be taken in by a complete stranger, without giving the least thought about Theodor. I could not do this, even if he wore six glasses one on top of the other. Now good night!"

The confusing muddle surging through Babet's head and heart would not permit her to be satisfied with Agathe's response. She needed a *confidante* right this moment, so although it was very late, she crept away to Victorine and found her still awake. To her dismay, she met the aunt there too.

With quick composure and levelheadedness and a little guile, she portrayed the meeting with Sir Charles and that he had mistaken her for Victorine as a funny joke. But instead of the hoped-for applause, the aunt sternly reprimanded her bold recklessness and asked her what she would do tomorrow when Sir Charles would meet the real Victorine and discover her deception! Dismally, Babet walked away without saying another word. In her lightheartedness, she had not thought of this.

Half in anger and half in fear, because the aunt's last comment had wounded her deeply, Babet wanted only to return to her room, but suddenly in the corridor she heard Angelika's harp music penetrating the stillness of the night. The need to talk to someone about what had happened that night was too great and propelled Babet towards Angelika, although in the past she did not usually take that serious girl into her confidence. Basically, she thought, Angelika was a good girl and an understanding one at that. Perhaps she can advise me on what I should do tomorrow morning so that I don't embarrass myself in front of everyone.

But poor Babet would not find a sympathetic ear this evening. Leaning against her harp, Angelika's face was very pale. She appeared to be willing to listen to Babet's energetic prattle in her usual quiet friendly manner but the words flew past her almost incomprehensibly. With great effort she struggled in vain to wrestle herself free from melancholy dreams that she preferred, to surrender to the solitude of the night. Unable to grasp the essence of Babet's words, Angelika's responses were so inappropriate and incoherent that Babet lost patience and finally left her to seek solace and advice from her pillow, the only *confidante* that remained.

In Babet, a very vivid imagination merged with an ice-cold disposition, a combination that occurs frequently in life. She had never had a serious thought in her life, but when she had lived at the boarding-house she had exhausted whole libraries. Those days, she sought change to relieve monotony and reading novels accelerated to a kind of passion for her. The little plots she needed to devise so that she could pursue this diversion unobserved heightened her pleasure considerably. She had come as a grown-up girl to her uncle's impressive home with her head full of the most intriguing adventures, and since an obsession with reading nothing but novels generally turns into a desire to play out the scenes of the novels, Babet now yearned to experience that which she had frequently read about. All her thoughts and wishes were focused on becoming a shining example of a heroine in a love story.

By coincidence, the student Theodor was the first person who gave her more attention than she was used to, so it was quite natural that she instantly imagined that she had discovered her hero. Babet did not realize that while he was living nearby, this young man Theodor had elected her to be queen of his heart, so as not to appear inept or unworthy; he was simply acting in a manner similar to most young men of his age. Overlooking this possibility, Babet instead began to act out a novel which actually only took life in her own head, although she may have denied this to Agathe.

Everything went well as long as the holidays lasted, but when they ended and Theodor returned to Göttingen the novel ended too. Babet was not even certain if she would see her beloved again, but he had left her with an over-stimulated fantasy and unmistakable vacuum, making the days somber and dull. For a while she consoled herself with an imaginary mourning for the distant beloved but she soon tired of this contrivance. She needed a new purpose to find happiness and so Sir Charles' appearance was most welcome at that moment. The grandeur that surrounded him and the hope that she would win his heart, though she was outmatched by the normally favoured Victorine, helped to flatter Babet's vanity. At the same time, her imagination was fired by his foreign ways and his unfamiliar personality.

Sir Charles' charm was perfectly suited for making a most agreeable impression on a young girl like Babet. You might say he was in fact a handsome man, although his entire being hinted at a weariness of life. The same kind of weariness we see too often today among our promising youth who spurn moderation to enjoy all of life's pleasures. The sagging in the regular features of his really quite pleasant face and the unnatural lethargy in his attitude, which he aspired to cultivate by adopting a fashionable indifference towards everything outside himself. gave him the aura of the quintessential hero. To Babet, he looked exactly like the heroes in the novels she had read.

In this first sleepless night of her life, she thought about him for a long time and repeated every word he had said to her and remembered his every look though she was oblivious to any presumptuousness, until she was convinced not only that she loved him, but that she had made a deep and positive impression.

That he, through no fault of her own, had taken her to be Victorine, she finally regarded from a most romantic perspective and she dismissed all the negative comments made by the aunt, even though just a short while ago these had filled her with anxiety. Finally, she persuaded herself that with the expected discovery of her true identity in the morning, she could only win, and now turned towards her wardrobe. She made a thorough inspection and finally chose the most becoming item for the big day tomorrow. It was almost daybreak when she finally fell asleep dreaming of Sir Charles and her new pink dress.

ENDNOTES

---

[1] A very intricate dance, where couples in square formation constantly shift partners.

[2] A popular 18th century social dance that preceded the quadrille.

[3] A member of a religious community of women.

[4] Pentecost is celebrated fifty days after Easter Sunday.

[5] June 24, a mid-summer related holiday.

[6] September 29, the feast of St. Michael.

[7] *Mater Dolorosa* is one of the three common artistic representations of a sorrowful Virgin Mary.

[8] A Prussian province from 1742 to 1945.

[9] A French term that in the 18th and early 19th centuries referred to the members of the lower middle social classes.

[10] The name Angelika (Angelica in English) is derived from the Latin *angelicus,* (angelic).

[11] The longest river in Germany.

[12] Angoulême is a city in southwestern France.

[13] A tropical plant with leaves that are sensitive to light or to touch.

[14] A voluntary force of the Prussian army, consisting mostly of students and academics from all over Germany, who had volunteered to fight against Napoleon I of France. The corps was named after Ludwig Adolf Wilhelm von Lützow.

[15] A spa town in Lower Saxony, Germany.

[16] Doctor of Law or Doctor of Laws is a doctoral degree in law.

[17] The office or room in which a business conducts accounting operations.

[18] Odessa is a major seaport located on the shore of the Black Sea, founded by the Empress Catherine the Great in 1794.

[19] In Greek mythology, nymphs are female divinities of lower rank.

[20] In the Holy Roman Empire, a free imperial city was a city formally ruled by the emperor only, whereas the majority of cities in the Empire were governed by princes of the Empire.

[21] A character in *L'Astrée*, a pastoral novel written by Honoré d'Urfé, published between 1607 and 1627.

[22] A long seat with a back, meant for accommodating more than one person.

[23] A traditional greeting whereby a girl or woman bends her knees while bowing her head.

[24] Christian Fürchtegott Gellert (July 4, 1715 – December 13, 1769). Gellert was a German poet, known for his didactic fables.

[25] A slow dance, of Polish origin. Music is played with the rhythm or style of a Polonaise.

[26] Johann Christoph Gottsched (1700-1766) was a German author and critic.

[27] Frederick II (1712-1786) was a King in Prussia from 1740 to 1772 and a King of Prussia from 1772 to 1786.

[28] A personal assistant to a queen, princess or noblewoman.

[29] *The History of Sir Charles Grandison*, was written by Samuel Richardson first published in 1753.

[30] Written by Johann Timotheus Hermes, (1738–1821), whose novels were

quite popular in the eighteenth century.

[31] Adam Gottlob Oehlenschläger (1779-1850) was a Danish poet and playwright. Correggio (1489-1534), was a painter during the Italian Renaissance.

[32] Unrivaled.

[33] *Der Frühling* is a poem written by Ewald Christian von Kleist 1715 – August 24, 1759.

[34] German poet (1724–1803).

[35] Caliban is a character is Shakespeare's play *The Tempest*.

> *Be not afeard; the isle is full of noises,*
> *Sounds, and sweet airs, that give delight and hurt not.*
>
> *Sometimes a thousand twangling instruments*
> *Will hum about mine ears; and sometime voices*
> *That, if I then had waked after long sleep,*
> *Will make me sleep again; and then in dreaming,*
> *The clouds methought would open, and show riches*
> *Ready to drop upon me, that when I waked*
> *I cried to dream again. (Act 3, Scene 2)*

[36] *Trißett* and *l'Hombre* were popular card games in the 18th century.

[37] Capital of Malta.

[38] *Annettchen* is a diminutive of Anna.

[39] In Greek mythology, Hydra was a multi-headed water monster.

[40] Principle floor of a large house.

[41] Fabric with a crimped appearance.

[42] Fine, often starched netting, frequently used for wedding gowns.

[43] Scottish-style dance.
[44] Lightweight, convertible carriage.
[45] Traditionally someone who is involved in the preparation of a wedding or in providing amusing entertainment.

www.ingramcontent.com/pod product compliance
Lightning Source LLC
Chambersburg PA
CBHW050128030726
47505CB00007B/2082